Freeman

Freeman

BY LILLIE D. CHAFFIN

THE MACMILLAN COMPANY
NEW YORK, NEW YORK
COLLIER-MACMILLAN LTD., LONDON

The Macmillan Company,
866 Third Avenue, New York, N.Y. 10022
Collier-Macmillan Canada Ltd., Toronto, Ontario

Library of Congress catalog card number: 78–187793

Printed in the United States of America

10 9 8 7 6 5 4 3 2 1

*To Phyllis Larkin
for all her infinite patience*

Freeman

1

Freeman tried to pretend he didn't see Billy Blackburn taking the short-cut path across the grass. Billy, however, had no intention of letting the matter drop. He motioned to G. C. Daniels, who was standing beside the highway. "Come on down." When G.C. didn't answer, Billy called, "You mean you're going to walk an extra half-mile twice a day to get to school because somebody thinks a path isn't pretty? Look up that hill at the cow paths, and you'll see they don't ruin anything. Come on." All the time Billy was walking toward Freeman, who was following the road from the lower end of the school grounds.

This was the second week of the second year at Prater Consolidated School, and Mr. Crowe was the second principal. Mr. Crowe had tried to find a job for everyone. One morning he had said over the intercom, "Clarence Coleman, G. C. Daniels and Freeman Sloan, it would be a favor to all of us if you'd be playground patrols. This, gentlemen, is a most important part of our total school program. The public sees and most often judges us by our outdoor housekeeping."

When the intercom clicked off, Clarence rolled his eyes at Freeman, held up his forefingers, crossed them and whispered, "We're supposed to work together like that."

G.C. and Billy lived up the hollow which began across the highway at the upper end of the school grounds. Freeman lived below the school. Billy's grandmother, Mag Blackburn, and Freeman's grandmother, Viney Sloan, were sisters, and sometimes Freeman wished he and Billy were as close as cousins ought to be. Neither had brothers and sisters, and the houses in the valley were far apart. But, for some reason unknown to Freeman, Billy often treated him more like an enemy than like a friend, especially when he was with G.C.

"What're you going to do about us tromping on the grass?" Billy asked as he came to a stop in front of Freeman.

Freeman took two backward steps and did not answer.

"I hear somebody tattled on us for leaving some bottles. You know something, a blabbermouth sooner or later meets his match. You've met yours, and you better not open that trap of yours to nobody. You think you'll ever get on the ball team like that and you've got more holes in your head than a flour sifter. Right now there's two bottles under the upper basket. Why don't you just go and pick them up like a good boy, Goody Sloan? And you can bring a pocketful of grass seed every day and walk along behind us, a kind of Freedy Grass-seed character. Might get your name in a history book or something."

The ball court was outside, since the school did not have a gymnasium. The basketball team was important to a lot of people in the school, and Freeman secretly longed to be part of it. Last year the team had won the sportsman trophy in the county tournament.

"Somebody can get hurt if the bottles get broken, you know," Freeman said lamely.

"Broken spoken, why don't you tend to your knitting?" Billy had been digging with his toe at a clump of grass. It came up, and he kicked it like a football.

G.C. looked down from his great bony height. "Touchdown. Yeah, why don't you go and make a report to the prin-ci-pal?"

"I've not made any reports. But you're on the patrol too, G.C.," Freeman said. "You should help or go in and resign, one."

"You think so?" When Freeman nodded, G.C. said, "And who do you think gives a mule's bray about what you think?"

A seventh-grade girl was walking past them with a candy bar in her hand. Billy grabbed at it. The girl gave him the candy, smiled and said, "Keep the change."

Billy crammed the candy into his mouth and said, "Wish I had me a candy factory. Freeman with that store's the next best thing, but his grandma keeps an eye on handing out samples. G.C., guess what I heard? That she's thinking of sending him off to a private school to keep him away from us naughty ones. Afraid we'll injure his ears. What time she's not got him cutting weeds and watering flowers she's got him tending that baggy-bones horse."

Freeman swallowed hard. He wanted to shout at Billy and defend Mom Sloan. He had lived with her almost since he was born, and she worked hard at giving him a good home. Nobody made Freeman tend to Old Nell. Tending her was a pleasure, for he loved her. And if horses loved people, Old Nell loved him. But all he said was, "Billy, leave me alone."

"Then don't ask for trouble, bud. I could squench you with my bare hands, but I don't want to have to wash so early in the morning. Too puny to do anything but dust them solid walnut chair rounds and pick petunias. While they roll in money from that grocery store and all."

Billy always talked loud and long when he was

with G.C. The Sloans' store sat by the side of the road, on the edge of the yard. One window was low, and there was a large space between the bars. Billy once had threatened to climb through the bars, and Freeman had been disturbed enough to tell Mom. She'd said, "You'll be a lot better off if you'll stay completely away from that boy. I'm going to call Mag and tell her how he's acting."

Billy clenched a fist now and swung it in a circle around Freeman's nose while G.C. spread his long arms so they circled Freeman's back.

G.C. cleared his throat, mocking a habit of Pop Sloan's. "Give the boy a hearing, man. You can't condemn a man without a hearing, I think. Maybe he'd like to run for Mr. Crowe's protective board of correction or his grandma's law of the tongue. You can't judge a pig by its poke."

Freeman turned. G.C.'s arms turned. He felt silly with Billy standing there circling that broad, plump fist around his nose. "If you don't stop—" He had no intention of hitting them; two against one would not have been good odds, even if they were not larger than himself. They probably wouldn't hit him. More than likely, they wanted him to say something they could report to the principal because they thought he was the principal's pet. He wished Mom hadn't made him carry that bunch of yellow mums to Mr. Crowe last week.

5

"You'll what?" Billy demanded. "Go on. Don't be bashful."

"That's a vague threat, man. It insinuates," G.C. said.

Desperately Freeman blurted out, "I'll give you a piece of my mind!" The minute the words were out, he was sorry. It was a stupid thing to say to them, but he hadn't taken time to consider the words, nor their possible effect. Mom had often told him it was impossible to take back anything once it was said, but he wanted to modify it and had opened his mouth when Billy's laughter rang out.

"Ho, ho, how-haw-hee. Hard up as you are, you'd better keep what mind you've got. None to trade on and none to spare for giving. You want a little piece of his mind, all caged up there in his little old skull, G.C., huh?"

"Nope, got more'n I can take care of already. Right?"

"Right." Billy nodded.

"And it's gone bad from not being used. Have to exercise your mind to keep it in order."

Billy pretended to be whispering in G.C.'s ear, but only a "buzz, buzz, buzz," came out. Billy laughed and rolled his big blue eyes, then said, "Buzz, Grandpa Bill Jack's a poor relation."

Mr. Crowe eased his car into the driveway and honked three times at the boys, who were now standing close together on the grass. A crowd had gathered, but it began to scatter at the first honk. If Freeman reported what had happened, the boys would be called to the office. They would accuse him of starting a quarrel.

As Clyde Daniels' bus pulled in with the last load of students, the bell rang. Freeman started immediately to Mrs. Philpott's sixth-grade homeroom. He wished he could ask for a transfer, away from Billy and G.C. But a transfer would only get him away from them part of the time. They might behave even worse on the playground.

Birdie Powell got off the bus just as Freeman reached the door. He waited for Birdie and pretended not to see Mr. Crowe standing in the office. As usual, Birdie was chewing gum, but he held it still until they were past Mr. Crowe.

Morning break was barely a break at all, since Mrs. Philpott was at the chalkboard explaining a math problem. And Prater School had a closed-lunch period: everyone went to the cafeteria together and then straight back to the classroom to begin work again. When the fifteen minutes of afternoon recess began, it was raining. Freeman stood outside Miss Goble's sixth-grade door and waited for Birdie.

Birdie peeked out and said, "Have to stay in. Lost my blasted English paper on the bus or somewhere."

Freeman walked to the end of the corridor and

stood looking outside. Billy came to stand beside him. Wind-blown, the rain hit the glass in silver icicles. The concrete walk was like the surface of a boiling pot, with raindrops swelling, bursting and then spreading out in layers.

Billy pressed his nose against a panel of the door and traced the wire that lay between the two layers of glass. "I guess this is a lot like being in prison, huh?"

"Could be."

Freeman was a little wary of committing himself with Billy. When they were alone, Billy often spoke to him in a friendly manner. But he also had the habit of remembering something Freeman said and making a joke of it later, when he had an audience.

Billy wiped fog from the glass. "Grandma got a letter from Chicago yesterday."

Billy's tone made a question of the sentence. It was like bait on a fishing line, as if he expected to catch something, maybe to draw Freeman into asking something. Freeman wished he could accept things Billy said as a way of passing time and of actually being friendly. Maybe they were. Billy was so changeable. But Freeman was changeable also, he had to admit.

"Was the letter from your dad?" Freeman asked when the silence kept growing between them and the recess noise kept getting louder.

"From my aunt. Bill Jack's girl. My Aunt Willie."

Again the words were really questions. You know I have an aunt? You know Bill Jack Coleman? You know anybody named Willie? You know we've got relatives in Chicago?

Freeman knew a lot of folks from Toms Creek had moved to Chicago, including Billy's father and, a long time ago, his own father and mother. But Mom and Pop never talked about the people who moved away and left their families. It seemed to hurt them to be reminded of those who deserted the land and broke family circles. Once Freeman had asked Pop about Billy's father, Big Bill, and Pop had answered, "I don't try very much to keep up with other people's business. Hear he's doing all right up there."

The bell rang and recess ended before Freeman thought of a suitable answer. "I knew you had some aunts, but I don't know their names."

During the ten minutes allotted for settling down and last-minute study before science class, Freeman thought about the first day he had gone to school. Mom had given him a piece of paper to give the teacher. Miss Grant had called his name and asked that he raise his hand. While his hand was in the air, she read aloud: "father, Fred Sloan; mother, Mae Sloan." He had stared at her open-mouthed, thinking Mom and Pop had names he hadn't known about. Mom's name was Viney and Pop's name was George. This was a mistake! Then Billy had called out, "He lives with his Grandpa and Grandma, just like I do."

Clarence Coleman said, "That's right."

Freeman wanted to deny this, but he was stunned and drew into himself to consider that Mom and Pop were not his parents. Why hadn't he known? Where were his mother and father? He was angry at Mom and Pop, then sad. He wanted to rush home and find out the truth. But he also wanted to wait, to watch them and see if they acted like parents or grandparents. He decided to wait. But that afternoon, as he watched Mom prepare dinner, he suddenly blurted out, "Mom, are you my grandparents?" His throat was dry. His eyes were dry also.

She was slicing potatoes into an electric skillet. She finished a potato before answering, "Yes."

"How come?"

"We just are."

"How come I didn't know?"

"We didn't tell you."

"Why didn't you tell me?"

"You were too small to understand."

"I'm not too small, not now." He waited for an answer, but she went ahead with shaking chicken in a brown paper bag, placing it slowly in hot cooking oil, salting it and covering it with a lid. He cleared his throat, the way Pop did when he was impatient for an answer. "Everybody knows more about everything than I do."

"Who's everybody, Freeman?"

"Billy and Clarence." So many questions wanted to come out at once that he began stammering. "If—if—if this Fred and Mae are my daddy and mother, why didn't you tell me? Where are they? Are they dead?" She hooked up the vacuum sweeper and he shouted, "Tell me!"

"I don't like to talk about it. Pop and I've tried to be parents to you and give you a good home. Yes, they're dead. Now just trust us, please, and don't go worrying about things that are long past."

Sweat and tears had made his face as soggy as the swamp below the barn. He wiped it on the tail of his new school shirt. Mom looked the same, only a little sadder. He kicked the side of the sink in his disappointment. He had wanted her to deny it! He had wanted her to explain that those names were hers and Pop's and that Billy and Clarence had been mistaken. He grabbed her about the waist and rubbed his face dry on her apron.

"Now, son," she said softly, slowly, as she loosened his hold. "You're squeezing me too hard. We love you. We need you. Pop and I'd be all alone if we didn't have you for our baby."

"I'm not a baby." He stretched tall. "I'm not your baby."

"Well, we'll still think of you as our baby, long as

we live, I guess. Why don't you go and rake some leaves off the yard?"

"Why didn't you tell me before now? And why don't you tell me what happened?"

"Because we didn't want you to be hurt. We wanted to wait for you to grow up awhile. I thought that teacher would write down the names instead of reading them aloud. Believe Mom, will you?"

He ran out and sat on the front steps until the disappointment and anger had settled in him, until they went down like the swelling when he struck his head against a stone.

He wasn't certain where her answer had divided into sentences. Had she said, "They're dead now. Trust . . ."? Or, "They're dead. Now trust"? He wanted to go back into the house and ask her what she had meant, but he felt he had upset her already. She was his mom, and she was trying to help him. She would tell him in time. There was no reason for being impatient and forcing answers. No reason for not waiting, except curiosity. But he would wait.

He grew tired of sitting, walked about scuffing the leaves. After a while he began raking them. Mom wouldn't lie to him.

"Whoa there, you're going to rake up all the grass," Pop said.

"Mom just told me my real daddy and mother

are dead." When Pop didn't say anything, Freeman said, "Are they?"

"Yes."

"How? How'd it happen?"

"It was an accident. Don't worry about it, son."

"Was my daddy your son?"

"Yes."

"Who was my mother, before she married my daddy?"

"A Coleman from Boldmans Branch."

Mom came to the door and asked, "Which would you boys rather have, chocolate pudding or ginger-bread?" Freeman knew there would be no more questions answered that day.

He thought of the late autumn day—it must have been a year later—when he and Billy had gone to gather beechnuts on the hill above Aunt Mag's house, across from the family cemetery.

Freeman had never been to the cemetery. If Mom had ever gone, she had not taken him or said anything about it. Billy told him the names on the stones, since he helped his grandmother cut weeds there each year before Memorial Day. A Fred Varney, an F. K. Varney, a Tansy Sloan, Baby Sloan, a George Sloan. "An accident," they had told him. Where were the graves?

He asked Mom about the graves that afternoon, the very minute he reached home.

"Son, I never told you they were up there. If they had been, we'd a decorated their graves together." She turned to the mixer and became very busy making a cake.

"Then where are they? Where are they?" he shouted, determined to be heard.

She turned away from him and wiped her face on her apron. "In Chicago. I thought maybe Pop'd told you."

"How'd it happen, Mom? I'm big enough to know. I am!"

"A gun. It hurts too much to talk about it. Why don't you peel us some onions, and we'll make a good kettle of homemade soup, the kind you like." She wiped her face again, muffling her voice. "The onions are in the cellar. It's so good and cool you can clean them down there and cool off yourself. And while you're there, see if I have any more of them sweet pickled apples Pop likes so much. I think there's one can. After supper, we better go pick up the last of those sweet apples and fix us up some more of those pickles."

Mrs. Philpott interrupted his thoughts by saying, "Freeman, I don't believe you'll learn much by holding your book upside down."

14

2

There was a baseball game on TV that evening. Pop liked country music and western programs, but he usually thought of a story for telling when he wasn't interested in the TV offering. Sometimes it was about his childhood, at other times an old folk tale.

His white hair lay against the black leather chair like snow on a mountain, and his hands played with the crocheted doilies on the arms of the chair as if he were plucking the strings of a banjo. Mom rested with some sewing, her basket on the floor between them, and her mind too busy with counting stitches or matching designs to allow herself to be drawn into the conversation. She concentrated so hard on what she was doing that often when she looked up her gray-green eyes had a distance in them, a little sadness and sometimes a touch of irritation that she had been called to leave the private world she kept at her fingertips.

Pop began, "I bet you've not heard the tale about

Jack and the Mule Skinner. Now, Jack he—"

Freeman leaned forward. "Is Bill Jack Coleman kin to us?"

Pop cleared his throat and wet his lips. "You're forgetting that it's not polite to interrupt."

Maybe it wasn't polite, and he didn't want to be rude, but Freeman needed an answer. He had no intention of being put off so easily. "Is he?"

Mom kept her eyes on the sweater she was knitting for Freeman. "I don't know what brought that on."

"We don't claim much kin. Billy was whispering some stuff to G.C. but he wanted me to hear."

"Pay as little mind to him as you can." Pop picked up a doily and held it. "You're ruining my story with this chitchat."

Pop had started the tale again before Freeman could repeat the question. They hadn't said yes or no. Bill Jack Coleman's name seemed to do something to them. If Mom and Freeman happened to be outside and Bill Jack passed, saying, "Howdy, folks," Mom would nod and turn her back to the road. If the large, one-armed man slowed his step or appeared about to speak again, Mom would send Freeman inside for a chore. If Pop were outside, he would say, "Howdy," in a dry, no-further-comment way. But if Bill Jack met Freeman alone on the road, he would reach for Freeman's hand and squeeze it or pat him on the back while saying, "How's things with you, boy?"

The handshaking and patting once happened before Freeman was quite out of sight of the house. That evening Mom had given him a little lecture on being too friendly with people. He had felt six inches tall and maybe six months old. "Any people, understand? Grownups. And there's no reason for going into a lot of why's. Just take my word for it, and some day you'll understand that everybody you know's not a friend."

While Pop talked on, Freeman's thoughts raced like the wind, here strong, there weak, then they'd strike Billy and blow strong again.

One day, when they were in second grade, Billy had been excited about Big Bill's coming home from Chicago for a visit.

"I bet you wish your dad'd come home," Billy had said. "I bet he would if he could."

"He can't, and you know it."

"Sure. I was just talking. Don't get your dandruff up."

"I didn't get my dandruff up. I just said he can't."

"It wasn't what you said. It was the way. Like you want to take your spite out on me or something. He's my kinfolks too."

Freeman waited for some further comment, but there was none. He became bold enough in third grade to ask G. C. Daniels, one day when Billy was absent, "Do you know anything about the accident that happened to my parents?"

G.C. smiled, then rolled his eyes and growled, "What accident? You don't be bugging me, Freeman Sloan. I don't know nothing about nothing, and why should I, when it doesn't concern me? If anybody'd know, it'd be your mom and pop."

Freeman didn't give up that easily. "You don't know a thing?"

"Not a thing." Then G.C. began to talk as if Billy were there and listening, or as if he were planning to tell Billy what had been said. "Anyway, what I know about anything's for me to know and you to find out the best way you can."

Freeman had walked away, found Birdie and begun a marble game which became so exciting he forgot how angry G.C. could make him, G.C. and Billy.

Another day, when he was about nine years old, Mom had found him looking through a drawer of the marble-topped dresser in the extra bedroom. She joined him and quickly took out everything: tie pins belonging to Pop, funeral brochures on Pop's family who had been struck by a train at the railroad crossing in Centerville, birthday cards, a peacock paper fan, some old photographs, yellowed and with worn edges. "Now that's it. No reason to be going through things and letting moths and bugs into them. There's not a thing in this entire house that you've not seen at one time or another. Hear now?"

There was a sternness in her manner that led him to say, "Yes, mam." What he really wanted to say was: "Where is everything else?" She would have said, "There is nothing else." She would not have said, "What else?" or "What do you mean?" She answered questions so there was no room for further questions.

There was no trace of his father and mother in the house—nothing. It was as though they had never existed at all. Surely there was something, something he could find. But Mom and Pop took him to a circus that afternoon, and he forgot his questions.

Once Billy had persuaded Freeman to go home with him after school. That also must have been when they were in second grade. Aunt Mag was in the creaky old swing on the front porch. She moved over with a playful groan and said, "Join me, pardner." She talked about her husband putting up the swing the week before he had been killed in a mining accident twenty years ago. While Billy fixed fried apple sandwiches, she pointed out flowers Will Blackburn had set, repairs he had made on the house.

"This is the old home place, and Viney probably thought it was her due, as the baby one, and George wanted it. Road went up here then, right over there." She pointed to a flat area now overgrown with small bushes. "Pa wanted me to have the house, on account of our having taken care of him. Viney and George talked him into letting her have all of the big bottoms and the highest hills with the most coal seams. Talked like she was doing me a favor by letting me keep all my land together. And they've got a fortune from the state for highways. George was working for the state highway department then and probably knew the road was going to be changed. And me like her own mother. It wouldn't have been anything but right for her to divide up with the heirs, all that coal and road and school house money that she'll be getting. But she never has divided, and she'll not."

Aunt Mag had spread her plump hands and put them together in an attitude of helplessness. "George said I'd hurt Viney's feelings and wasn't being fair. They took the first batch of money and built that big barn of a house too fancy for my blood. Because she taught school three years, way back, she's always thought she was better'n most people. Always sour as a pickled prune when I told her how I felt." She sighed. "Out of all my seven children, Billy's daddy's the only one divorced and double married. But Billy—there he is now—Billy, I was telling Freeman what a little blessing you've been to Grandma."

"Oh baloney," Billy said. "Feel of my back there."

Aunt Mag ran her hand up and down his back. "I don't feel anything."

"Just wanted you to see I wasn't sprouting any wings."

"Viney's always had her store. Credit's going to put them out of business though. Don't want to upset anybody by pushing for debts to be paid." She said to Billy, "We're going to have to have Freeman come up here more often and visit us poor relations. They keep him there like a bird in a cage. A fine cage doesn't always turn out a fine feathered bird, though."

"Freeman!" Pop called from a lilac bush below the house. "Freeman? There you are, and it's time for supper. Hello, Mag. How are you?"

"Can't complain. If I did, nobody'd listen. You're a rank stranger up this hollow, George. Come on in and tell me the latest."

Pop moved only a step or two forward on the clean-swept path. "Better get back. We've been getting the potatoes and early corn planted. That lilac bush smells good. Viney never did get one to take hold and grow down at our place."

"Takes free-hearted people to have green thumbs,

21

George. Remind me next spring and we'll get her another sprout."

When Freeman lagged, Pop called, "Hurry on, son."

Freeman would've liked to stay longer and listen to Aunt Mag talk. It was nice talking with Aunt Mag, but it was really even nicer to be going home.

As they walked, Pop had cut a large willow branch and made a whistle, then they gathered some pussy willows for Mom. "They'll tickle your mom. And now, buddy boy, don't you make a habit of going off anywhere without permission to do so. Home's the best place to be, and we worry when you're not there."

That evening Freeman had pulled a footstool near Mom and leaned back against her legs. Looking up, he could see the sag of her chin, the wrinkles and brownish streaks on her forehead. He had not thought of her as old until that minute.

"Son," she'd said, giving him a playful push, "go over there and sit on Baby Bear's chair. You're mashing my old bones. We put you out a few of those good green beans today, and some radishes." He'd rubbed his head against her, rolled over and imagined that the hair-line crack in the ceiling plaster was Mom's face. Only that crack-face had a smile, really a laugh like a jack-o'-lantern. Mom didn't often smile. She didn't frown either. She just looked sad or solemn, and he wanted to make her laugh. He laughed.

"Something's got his funny bone." Mom poked him in the ribs. "Now go on over and let me rest. And, Freeman, you worried me something awful, going off like that. Don't you go home from school with anybody unless you get permission."

"Would you have given permission?"

"Probably not."

"Why?"

"Because I know you're safe when you're home."

Aunt Mag's house was the closest one in either direction, and it was a half mile away. Mom said the highway was too dangerous, with more cars and trucks on it every day and the railroad crossing it every mile or so. She also said that people were busy and didn't really want to be bothered with visitors very often.

"Billy asked me. He invited me," Freeman had protested.

"Billy's not the entire boss. And sometimes people just say 'you-all come' to be polite. It's considered being polite to ask people to visit, and if they're visiting uninvited to ask them to eat with you, but lots of times they don't really mean it. It's like when people say 'how are you?' they don't really want you to tell them all your ailments or your troubles."

It just never seemed to come around to the right time for Freeman to invite friends home. Only if a boy came to the store did he have a chance to play for a while. Still, he hadn't exactly been suffering in unbroken silence and longing. Pop took him fishing and hiking. He had Old Nell and the dogs. He had good books to read, and he liked reading. They went to a drive-in movie often in summer.

Freeman's thoughts stopped abruptly as Pop came on strong with the ending of the tale. "And Jack said, 'Thank you kindly, sir' as he walked off with that there mule."

Freeman wished he hadn't let his mind wander so. Pop's stories were interesting, and he usually enjoyed them. He was about ready to comment on the story, to say, "Tell how the trade went again," when Pop got up and went to the kitchen for a drink.

When Pop returned, he said, "Trouble brewing up Jims Fork. Hatler Collins says that they'll not strip his land for coal. He went by when I was out fixing the slat on the fence." Pop didn't see Mom shaking her head at him. "Said he'd stop them dozers with a dose of lead, or lay down and they'd have to run over him. They're getting up a petition, he said, and asking everybody to sign it saying they want strip mining outlawed."

"Maybe we'd better stay out of it, George. We've got no kick on the mines. If they strip that hill over there, it won't hurt much, if they sow it back in grass like they're supposed to."

There had always been a pistol on the wall of Mom's and Pop's bedroom. It had belonged to Pop's dad, and Pop took it down once or twice a year to oil and clean it. It was never loaded, but there were shells in a chest drawer. They never allowed Freeman to use it and warned him never to touch it when they were away.

"Why don't you teach me to shoot?" Freeman asked now.

Pop shook his head. "Don't know that I could shoot it myself. It just kind of gives a feeling of protection to have a gun about the place, in case you ever need it. But if this one didn't belong in the family, I'd probably not have one."

"I'm about the only boy on the creek without a gun. Billy's got a rifle, got it for his birthday. I've never even had a toy gun. I don't see why you have to treat me this way."

He saw Mom's face freeze, and he was immediately sorry. He knew that she hated guns, even hated the word. He wanted to tell her that he hadn't meant all he said, but Mom wasn't much for apologies. Once she'd said, "Saying and doing's two different things. You prove you're sorry by the way you act, not by saying so. And when you wish you hadn't said or done something, you have to live it down.

It takes so much time, apologizing and living things down, that people ought to think for a long time before they say something or do something which may hurt themselves or others."

Pop shook his head. "We treat you the best we know how. Son, pioneers needed guns. In the early days, you never knew when or how you'd have to protect yourself. People hunted for food and also for hides for selling. But if there were fewer guns in the world now, the world'd be better off."

Hoping to make amends by changing the subject, Freeman said, "Gee, Mom, my sweater's going to be great."

The diamond-patterned sweater was going to be very nice. Letting Mom know that he thought so might help her to forget the stupid complaint he had made about the gun. He really didn't want a gun very much anyway; only the fact that they had always denied one to him made it seem attractive. Bill Jack Coleman had lost an arm to his own gun while hunting. A man at the mouth of Jims Fork had lost a foot while cleaning a gun he thought wasn't loaded. Very few good things could come from owning one, and he'd never want to kill animals for entertainment.

"Hadn't that confounded ball game ought to be off? Freeman, see if you can pick up 13. Maybe we'll get some different commercials we can enjoy."

Except for rare occasions when the signal changed or the antennae on top of the hill blew around, they only got Huntington's Channel 3, the Tri-State Channel. If they could only get one channel, they preferred 3 because it gave more news of Eastern Kentucky.

They lapsed into silence, with the TV turned up loud, the way Mom and Pop preferred it. The noise suddenly separated them and made the house big and cold and empty. You couldn't ask questions above the noise, and if you did they could always pretend not to hear them.

Freeman wasn't interested in the quiz game. He felt restless and unhappy. With a sigh, he picked up the book which had been in the brass basket beside his chair. The chewing gum wrapper he was using to mark his place reminded him of Birdie Powell.

"Get me some gum when you're in the store next time," he said to Mom. He held up the wrapper, and she nodded.

Pop turned to lie down on the couch. "If you're swallowing all that gum, you must be planning on setting up a rubber plantation," he teased. "Mom said the other day that she never did see any sticking around on things."

3

The next day began like any other day, as much as one day can be like another. Freeman dressed before going downstairs to the huge breakfast Mom made each morning.

It began being different when he said at the foot of the stairs, "I don't want anything to eat."

"That's the way to keep from getting hungry. A good bed, good food, peace and quiet, clean clothes and plenty of fresh air and exercise're what it takes to have a healthy body," Mom said.

When Freeman began trying to fit a piece into the puzzle on the coffee table, Pop said, "Come on now and mind your mom."

Freeman had forgotten to bring down his notebook, and after two hot biscuits, an egg and two slices of ham, he dashed back upstairs.

"Brush your teeth," Mom called.

He wished she didn't feel she had to remind him to wash his hands before eating, brush his teeth after eating, drink all his milk, chew with his lips closed, and on and on, as if he didn't have any idea of what he should do. True, he did forget at times, and at other times he decided there wasn't any need for a particular action, but he wasn't a baby any more.

His high-cheek-boned face was so familiar he stood before the mirror and brushed his teeth without noticing a smudge of egg yolk on his chin. He gave one rake with a wet comb at the cowlick on his forehead, then ran to his room, skidding on the green nylon rug Mom kept on the polished bit of floor between the bathroom tile and the hall runner. He smoothed a corner of his bedspread and stacked a stray recording beneath the record player. He unplugged his radio, thinking of taking it to school for Mr. Crowe, in case he wanted to listen to the University of Kentucky versus Eastern University game, but decided someone would say "Brownie points" or "Apple polishing"—that someone being either Billy, G.C. or Clarence.

Sunlight reflected on the fish bowl, half-filled with cat-eye marbles, that sat on the window sill. He had so much. And he was ashamed of himself for feeling, as he had last night, that he had nothing. "Being lucky," Pop had said one time when they were fishing and had caught a big catfish, "is in knowing you're lucky. If we'd wanted only trout, we'd be able to feel unlucky, if we wanted to." Freeman felt lucky this morning. He didn't want anyone to change that feeling.

At the foot of the stairs he called, "Mom, they're fixing breakfast at school now. Good, they say, and real cheap. If you and Pop'd like to sleep later, I could eat up there. How about it?"

"Can't sleep late after the habit of getting up early for years. Birds frolic in the mimosa outside my window and wake me. I don't mind it, don't mind it at all."

"Maybe Pop'd like to watch some late programs?"

"Your pop's not all that interested in late programs. He's an early bird too. You're not feeling puny, are you?"

Freeman went through the large dining room, which served only as a hallway from the living room to the kitchen. The big table, with its sides folded down, was pushed against the window and held a collection of violets. He picked up his lunch bag and shook his head. "As Pop says, I feel fine as frog hair."

Pop was still at the table, finishing his coffee. "Be careful now and come straight home. And if you don't wipe your chin, somebody'll think you're advertising eggs."

After supper that evening, Freeman sat on the roof of the barn and watched a coal truck turn the curve above the house. In the clear light, the black truck with its black load made the big weather-boarded house look even whiter than it was. From where he sat, the store building looked as if it were fastened to the house.

Brakes squawked when the truck turned off the main road and cut across the creek behind the house. The load tilted to the right side and a shovelful of coal spilled onto the ridge that had been building up for the month the new dock had been in operation. He watched the truck back up the ramp, but before the bed lifted to dump the coal he was lost in thought. When the truck came down the ramp, he realized his eyes had been turned toward the hill but he had not been looking at anything.

This morning Billy had said, "Here," and given him the letter he'd mentioned the day before. For the rest of the day Billy and G.C. avoided him, as if Billy thought Freeman should come and thank him. But the letter had been like a puzzle with some important pieces missing. He found it interesting, but he couldn't decide why it had been given to him. What was back of Billy's actions?

The letter began, "Dear Maggie and Family," and then rambled on with two pages of news concerning Aunt Mag's three sons who lived in Chicago. "Bill is hoping he can persuade Billy to come up here and live with him." That sentence was underlined with a broad, scrubby pencil. Had Billy meant to brag about this? Like, I may leave soon? Or, somebody besides Grandma cares for me? Then it said, "If you see George and Viney, tell them I asked about them. And Poor Freeman, he looks so lonely. Give him my love, Maggie. The day I've been hoping for is getting closer. I'll be calling." "Poor Freeman" had been underlined also. The signature began with an enormous W and trailed off into a series of curves and straight lines, which Freeman supposed made the name Willie, since Billy had said the letter was from his Aunt Willie.

What could Billy hope to gain by passing Aunt Mag's mail around? He hadn't said anything about wanting it back, about reading between the lines—nothing except "here." Aunt Mag would almost surely want to keep the letter. She was a keeper of things, and a history of Toms Creek could probably be found in the old boxes and barrels and trunks scattered from cellar to attic, from smokehouse to barn. Maybe Billy wanted to rub "Poor Freeman" into some wound he suspected Freeman had. Perhaps Freeman should have opened it immediately, read the greeting and handed it back with, "Thanks, but this isn't mine." But Billy had handed it to him furtively, behind a book, as he went to his seat, and Freeman had accepted it in the same manner, placing it in his shirt pocket until the class was well under way. Even then, he should have given it back, instead of sticking it back in his pocket. Whatever Billy had on his mind, let him be disappointed.

Freeman remembered hearing Mom and Aunt Mag talking once, and Mom had said, "Now, Sister Maggie, you just leave me and my family out of your letters." Mom's voice had been soft and kind, but Aunt Mag had answered sharply, "Then I'm done with you, Sister Viney."

"Every time things don't go to suit you, you're done with me, Mag. It suits me to a T."

Aunt Mag's voice rose even louder: "No use wasting my breath talking to a stone wall."

And Mom's voice rose a little: "My opinion exactly. That's why I don't talk more. Least said's soonest mended, and you tell Billy to stop pestering Freeman. Acts like a rooster pecking a newly hatched chick. And I don't want him and Billy trading pictures. I washed my hands long ago."

Aunt Mag snorted loudly and said, "And that makes you no more innocent than Pilate." Later Freeman had looked up Pilate in a dictionary, but he couldn't see any possible connection between Mom and Pilate.

Aunt Mag had left saying, "I'll be back when you send after me, and not until, Viney Sloan, my baby sister." She said the last part of the sentence as if it were something so ugly that she no longer intended to claim it.

"Don't hold your breath," Mom answered, "and when I need somebody to look after my business, I'll hire someone."

After that Aunt Mag didn't visit very often, and she didn't let Billy come to visit at all. When she was there, Mom always sent Freeman out to do a chore, but he could hear Aunt Mag griping and arguing. Never anything that made much sense. "She just likes to hear her head rattle," Mom had said good-naturedly when Freeman asked why Aunt Mag fussed so much.

Freeman backed down the log walls of the barn and went to the stall where he had hidden the letter in a feed box under a pair of old leather gloves and some hay. He could not have explained why he had hidden it. For some reason, he had felt he should keep it safely for a while and think about what Billy thought the letter should mean to him. He never knew when Mom might decide to begin tidying every drawer and every corner of his room, even turning the mattress on his bed. He didn't want to have to try and explain, if she should find it.

The hall of the barn was dim and the ground was spongy as a carpet. It was always a little spooky in the late afternoon and evening, filled as it was with spiders and rats and beetles. The feed box was nailed in a far corner of the stall. In his hasty attempt to hide the letter, he had closed the stall door, which was a mistake. If Pop had come to the barn for anything, he would have checked to see why the door was closed. Of course, he wouldn't have looked in the feed box, not unless it looked strange. Freeman lifted the wooden latch and let his eyes adjust to the cool dimness.

A slithering sound made him hold his breath and wait for a longer look before moving again. A fat black snake was resting on the top log, in the middle of the stall, its head moving rhythmically, back and forth, up and down. Pop knew black snakes were in the barn, and he didn't want them disturbed because he said they fought away poisonous copperheads and rattlers. Still, Mom wasn't convinced that black snakes were entirely safe and was always warning Freeman to be careful. He wasn't completely sure of the snake himself and he stepped warily across the floor, watching the snake and watching the path he would take.

There was nothing to use for lifting the straw, so he grabbed it out by quick handfuls until he reached the letter. He backed out of the stall, his heart beating heavily and his breathing fast, a little ashamed of his fear, folding the letter to fit his hip pocket and buttoning the pocket on it.

Freeman was standing at the lane gate, stroking

Old Nell's forehead, when Pop came to the lower end of the garden to gather a squash. "Think I'll take a short ride," he called to Pop.

The horse rolled her eyes and snorted a little when he put the bridle on her, but when he jumped onto her bare back she started walking quietly. He clucked a couple of times to get her near enough for him to open the gate that separated the pasture land from the truck road. Old Nell wasn't used to going up the creek and she shied to the left as they passed the coal dock. Once past it, she needed no further encouragement, and he let her choose her own direction. She sniffed the garbage burning at the back of the school grounds and stepped a bit faster to be rid of the smell. A few yards past the school, a crow flew across their path. Old Nell shook her head, turned from it and went up Colemans Creek.

Freeman had been busy watching a rainbow, and they had gone several yards before he noticed that they had left the nearly dry stream bed and were following a narrow road around the side of a hill. Freeman had been up this road only once. He and Billy had been catching minnows in a bucket when a rainstorm came up. They were wet before they found shelter under a cliff, where Goober Coleman was lying on his stomach and tossing pieces of slate at a sycamore a hundred feet or so down the hill. Goober was Bill Jack's grandson, come to visit from

Cincinnati. He had been catching crawdads, and he and Billy had begun an argument about crawdads biting and holding on until it thundered.

Now a dog ran from behind a junked car and began snapping and growling at Old Nell's heels. "Get off! Go on!" Freeman shouted.

The dog slowed, bared its teeth, then sidled off toward the big two-story log house on the right side of the road, farther up the hill. The sound of hammering reached Freeman just as Old Nell decided to follow the dog. A skeleton of a room had been added onto the upper end of the house, the yellowish two-by-fours contrasting sharply with the grayness of the logs. At the back of the skeleton, Freeman could see the outline of a man, evidently working on a window casement for the new addition.

"Here, Tige, you better be back there resting," the man scolded. It was Bill Jack Coleman. "Stop that fool barking and tend to your business." Other dogs joined in from back of the house.

Bill Jack came to the front and stood in an opening that might be a door when the structure was completed. "Light down and rest your saddle. You're not lost, are you?"

As Freeman dismounted, Clarence came around the upper corner of the building with a roll of tar paper on his shoulder. He set the load against a post.

"Well, do look at what the cat's dragged in, or was it the dog? How'd you ever get this far-off?"

"Clarence!" Bill Jack shouted. "You hush that before I take a board to your setdown, and I don't mean maybe."

Freeman couldn't pinpoint the minute or the conversation when he'd learned it, but he knew that Bill Jack had been in prison once for making and selling whiskey. Anyway, it didn't matter to him. Bill Jack had always been nice to him. He knew that Clarence was Bill Jack's son by a third wife, and nobody, it seemed to Freeman, cared much for Clarence, but that was because of Clarence's sharp tongue and not for any reason connected with his family.

"Old Nell just came this way. We started out, and I let her choose directions," Freeman said.

Bill Jack nodded. "Smart horse."

Clarence tore some pages from a catalog lying on the ground and fanned himself. "Freeman Sloan, in the flesh. I bet he sneaked off. Bet a nickel they don't know where he's at."

Bill Jack moved the roofing to the doorway. "I bet a nickel you don't even have a nickel. Did, it'd burn a hole in your pocket. You go and get that putty for the window glass and some tacks for the roofing. What really brought you up this way?"

Before Freeman had time to answer, Bill Jack

walked closer, squinting against the sun. "Be careful on the highway. Them coal trucks are apt to make a horse skittish, especially one's not been on the road much."

Freeman led Old Nell on up the steep clay hill. He had come this far. Maybe he had meant to come here when he started. He didn't have time to lead up to any questions, even if he knew what the questions should be. Mom and Pop would be getting worried, and Bill Jack had work to do. Mae Coleman from Boldmans Branch. Coleman. There were a lot of people with the name, just as there were a lot of people named Sloan.

"Could I ask you a question or two?" Freeman was a little surprised at his own boldness, and he patted Old Nell to hide his shyness.

"Fire away. But I don't know that I can give you any answers. Never went far in school. Only moved once in my born days, so I've never traveled far in the world."

What had he meant to ask? He had asked if he could ask and now he had to say something. "Well, Mom and Pop Sloan are my grandparents, but I can't get them to tell me anything."

Bill Jack reached for his hand and squeezed it. "They're trying their level best to take care of you. You listen to them." He released the handshake and scratched the puckered flesh on his other arm where the hand was missing. "If I'd listened to my ma, I wouldn't a gone hunting that wet day and slipped on the leaves and blowed off my hand. Been paying for that ever since. Now, from all I hear, they're real good to you. Give you nigh about everything. And the way they feel's that you're all they've got. Boy, you let good enough alone, hear?"

"But they won't tell me about anything. About—"

"No abouts. Everything adds up to a real good home for you. You don't have to scratch for a living, grubbing the hills for herbs and skinning animals to pay for bread. Sunup to sundown, I've had to do it. And some of it because of my own bad judgment. You're sitting on top of a good world, and you just stick right with it, hear?" Bill Jack took up a hatchet, held it against his body with the crippled arm and began filing the edges.

"But Clarence and Billy and people keep hinting. I guess it's about the acci—"

"Wait till I give them a piece of my mind and if that don't work, I'll tan their dog hides."

"Mom and Pop told me long ago that there was an accident. But they won't tell me anything else."

"That's right. That's what I heard. They'd only do right by you, and you stop chomping at the bits. Can't nobody in their right mind have any kick on them trying to raise you up right, and right good."

"Supper's ready. Supper," a woman called.

Bill Jack laid down the tools quickly, as if he were

glad for the interruption. "I better get in there in a hurry. Cassie gets riled if I don't jump to the table when she says eat. Be dark soon, and you better not be on the road after dark. Lights might scare your horse."

The woman came to the door. "Didn't know you had company."

"He's leaving."

"Welcome to come in and eat with us," she called loudly.

"Thank you, but I've eaten." Clarence came around the corner with a box. There would be no further chance for talking, Freeman knew. "Old Nell and I'd better be getting back." He waited, hoping the others would go away and he could speak to Bill Jack again.

"You be careful now," Bill Jack called as he went into the house.

Freeman hadn't said what he wanted to say, and he hadn't received any answers. Bill Jack had kept interrupting him, kept praising Mom and Pop.

Clarence called, "Need me to help you climb on that baggy bones?"

"Clarence," Bill Jack called, "you come to supper this minute." Clarence went inside and Bill Jack said, "Put your foot in your mouth every time you open it. If I hear . . ." His words trailed off as they went into another room.

Freeman led Old Nell down the hill. At the creek,

he climbed onto her back and let her go at her own speed toward home. He liked the feel of the horse under him, warm and firm. At the barn, he hung the bridle in the stall and left the horse free in the barn lot. Before leaving, he patted her and spoke to her. "It was a nice ride, and I'm not going to tell Mom and Pop where we went. We just went for a ride, didn't we? If they hear about it, then I'll try and explain." Maybe this was the way they felt, the reason they kept putting off telling him about the accident. But knowing that he didn't know hurt. They had to tell him soon.

At the kitchen door, Freeman wiped his feet. Then he plunged through the dark kitchen and dining room as if the black snake were after him. The living room was bright with Mom's lamp and the TV. She dropped a handful of green beans into a pan, making a dull thud.

She finished a sentence she'd begun, ". . . save us all some worry. Where you been, son?"

"Rode up the creek, past the schoolhouse."

Pop groaned a little as he turned on the couch. "Bring me a drink, will you? We were just talking about Old Nell. You don't ride her much any more. And she's not eating enough, getting thinner every day. We were thinking . . ."

"I feed her. She eats some of it," called Freeman from the kitchen as he took a glass from the top of the refrigerator and filled it with ice water. He waited impatiently until Pop finished drinking, then reached for the glass.

"I may want it again," Pop said, setting the glass on the polished floor.

"Ruin the floor. Set it on the rug." When Freeman started toward the stairs, Mom asked, "Where you going?"

"Thought I'd read for a while."

"Don't wallow up the bedspread. I just washed it. The way that picture's flashing on and off, we must be going to get that predicted storm."

He had the letter unfolded and was getting ready to read it when Mom called, "Freeman, you got one of my good glasses. Come and put it back. You know where the everyday glasses are."

He dropped the letter on the bed and hurried to put the glass away. There was a good smell he hadn't noticed before. He found gingerbread on the stove and took a square of it, then rinsed the glass and set it in the rack in the sink. A great slam at the dock caused him to go back to the window. A truck was turned so that its lights showed a winch line being attached to a dozer, then a truck being drawn up from the creek.

"What's going on over there?" Mom asked from where she was kicking down the corner of a rug at the foot of the stairs. "Wind's getting awfully loud.

George, maybe you'd better turn that TV off. Lightning struck Mag's set and burned it out, she told me this morning."

"When?" Pop asked.

"That storm last night, oh, about midnight."

"That clay must've been slick," Freeman said. "Truck slid into the creek, and a dozer's pulling it back onto the road."

When he reached his room, the letter was gone. He remembered dropping it on the bed. Maybe it had slid across the bed and onto the floor. He walked to the foot of the bed, heaved against it, and moved it another inch or so from the wall. He crawled around the bed and peered under it. Although he couldn't remember trying to hide the letter, he stuck his hand under the pillows, lifted the bedspread and the quilt, patted his pockets. The window was closed, so it couldn't have blown outside. Maybe he had—although he was certain he hadn't—left it downstairs.

"Thought you planned to read," Mom said when they met on the stairs.

"Viney," Pop said in a tone that meant "leave him alone." Bending over the stair rail, Pop continued, "You know tomorrow's Phillips's day up the creek here."

Freeman went into the kitchen and cut another slice of gingerbread. He could hear the sound of

Pop's voice going on but not the words. Taking an everyday drinking glass, he poured a drink of cold water from the pitcher, then felt on top of the refrigerator. The letter wasn't in the kitchen. Mom had been at the foot of the stairs when she asked about the noise the truck and dozer were making. If she'd been upstairs, she'd found it. That must be it.

Freeman took the stairs two at a time. He stamped his foot on the scatter rug in front of the bathroom. There was nothing he could do. It wasn't her letter; it also wasn't his. It would take too long tonight to try to explain why he had accepted it, why he had kept it. And she'd probably say, "How do you know it's not something Billy Blackburn cooked up just to tantalize you? Maybe to try and get you to beg him not to go off to Chicago, or to tell me so that I'd ask Mag about it, or something?"

Flashes of lightning lighted the room and thunder sounded as if some heavy object were being moved across the sky, the way the house sounded if he were downstairs and Mom upstairs housecleaning. Then rain lashed the windows. That stupid Billy! Aunt Mag hadn't given him the letter. And it wasn't really all that important. Poor Freeman. Billy had given it to him because it said "Poor Freeman." Maybe. Where did Mom put things to make them disappear? Fred Sloan couldn't have grown up in this house without having toys and books and papers. Pictures, too. Maybe the photographers didn't come to school every year back then. Still, they would have taken him to Centerville and had pictures made, surely. Maybe they didn't have much money then for pictures.

Freeman threw himself heavily on his bed. "Pop, I just now remember that I didn't see Old Lead and Stemper at the barn."

"Yeah? Well," Pop said.

Freeman expected Mom to say, "Bread eaters." She often said it, not because she disliked the dogs or begrudged Pop their companionship. It was just something to say. And she indulged him with hunting dogs he never used any more, just as he accepted her sewing things they didn't really need. She said, "You didn't sound disturbed. Where are they?"

"Let Clarence Coleman take them this morning. Said he was going hunting and their dog got snakebit." After a while, Pop said, "Viney, don't be that way. Can't we let bygones be? We're going to have to think some things over and make some decisions."

"He had his way, signing that paper."

Pop's voice was muffled, as if he were talking behind his hand or with his head under the cover. "Nearly . . . years . . . can't . . . now . . ."

"I'm not going to let anybody force us into doing something."

"We can't put it off much . . . no matter how we feel . . ."

Freeman lay so still his breathing sounded like a windstorm, but the sentences kept trailing off, kept being covered up. Then they were asleep, leaving only bits of sentences to gouge at the darkness. He'd listened many days and nights, but he'd never heard much.

One night last week he'd been reading a mystery story by moonlight and Mom and Pop had thought he was asleep. He was getting sleepy when he'd heard Pop say, "Viney, we're not always right." Mom had given a long sigh and said, "You had as much to do with all decisions as I did." Then Pop answered, "I know I did. I said 'we.' Maybe you should've argued with some of my decisions." Mom said in a lower voice, "We said we wouldn't talk about it. I can't get over him signing the paper. Signing a paper with a lie on it and marrying her off at fourteen, and him knowing we hoped . . . college. I can't talk about it. My Lord, she wasn't much older than Freeman is right now." Freeman had closed the book, hoping to hear more. The bedsprings had squeaked and then there was silence. He had sat holding the book, waiting, wondering, as he wondered now.

4

Each morning Mom Sloan packed Freeman's lunch. The few times he forgot to bring it to school she sent it to him. If he ate it or gave it away before lunch time he was so disappointed in the cafeteria offering that he wished he could ask for his own lunch back. Friday's menu read: hot dogs, peas, potatoes, fruit cup, butter and milk. The fruit cup was ten or twelve raisins on a saucer.

Those with their own bags and boxes saved seats for friends who were creeping along in line for a plate from the cafeteria. Questions were loud: "Want my cold dog?" "Shove the mustard, please." "Who wants my gluey potatoes?" Comments were a little lower. "Oh, dig this giant cup of fruit." "Frozen wiener, stale bun make a hot dog delish."

When Freeman motioned, Birdie Powell sneaked away from Miss Goble's lunch line to join him. Billy, sitting nearby, salted and peppered his raisins, lined them along the wiener and added a generous spoonful of mustard from the jar on the table. "A den of thieves," he said, reaching across the table and adding a row of Freeman's potato chips to the mustard. When Freeman pretended not to notice, he said, "Say, what's ailing you, Freedy? Act like you got the pure punys here lately. Face long as three days of rainy weather. You do look lonely, boy." He raised his voice and tried to sound like a woman.

"Nothing's wrong with me, Billy boy. Nothing to say, nothing said's a good policy." He turned to Birdie and offered half of his spiced ham sandwich and one of the cakes from the plastic twin pack.

Billy whistled, rolled his eyes and said, "Stingy, I do declare it don't pay to have rich kinfolks, don't pay a-tall." He grabbed at the potato chips, causing Freeman to drop them on the floor. He saw Birdie looked displeased about it. "And what're you going to do about the present world situation, dear old classmate?"

Birdie bit into the cake and left a rim of marsh-mallow and chocolate on his upper lip. "I was just thinking how I'm going to hit your elbow and send that mess all the way down to your gizzard if you keep it up."

"Listen to that child, trying to pretend he's from the city because he went to Detroit this summer. Like he doesn't know my gizzard's full and so's my craw." He flipped a mustardy raisin at Birdie, but it landed on the front of Freeman's shirt.

Freeman brushed it off, smearing the mustard. "Stop it. You want to eat like a pig, go join a pig pen."

"Pardon me. Thought that's where I was at. Anybody'd wear a white shirt to this banquet needs his head examined and his neck and shoulders."

He reached for the bag of peanuts Freeman had laid on the table just as Freeman started to say the shirt was beige-colored. Birdie slapped Billy's hand, as if he were playing a game. Billy moved from the next slap and dropped the sodden mess of bread, meat, mustard, potato chips and raisins onto his plate.

"How about a pea?" Billy threw a loose pea onto Birdie's sandwich.

Birdie threw the pea back at Billy. Billy dodged, knocking the plate onto his lap. Peas and raisins flew across the table, striking other students who joined in. Mrs. Philpott, at the table reserved for teachers, got up and descended on them. She grabbed Clarence Coleman, who was the nearest one, and shook him.

"What's going on here?" she asked, still hanging onto Clarence's shoulder. "Can't trust you to eat without some kind of trouble. All of you get up from there and start cleaning up this mess immediately."

G.C. had been seated three places from Billy and had been trying to get another boy to trade places with him. Now he managed, in getting up, to knock a plate to the floor. Around and around it spun, in large circles and small ones, until it struck a fork beside one of the three garbage cans and settled with a flat thud. Freeman stepped on a mound of potatoes and stood holding up his heel as if he were crippled. Everyone seemed frozen in whatever positions they had taken when the plate began traveling.

"Who started this?" Mrs. Philpott glared at all of them in turn. No one answered. "Then every one of you's responsible. Take your plates and empty them and throw away any bags. Lunch is over. I want this cleaned up completely in five minutes. Get some rags and mops."

Freeman wiped his shoe with a napkin and grabbed a plate. Clarence took it from him. "Hold on, smarty. That's my wiener and I'll take care of it." Clarence stuck the wiener in his mouth, like a cigar, and chewed on it as he swiped food into a pan.

Billy scrubbed a broom up and down in the potatoes and milk, as if he were mixing cement. "Instead of giving this to the janitor's hogs, we could go out and repair the highway."

Mrs. Philpott, with her hands on her hips, glared at Billy and commanded, "Shovel that into the garbage. G.C., you get a mop. A clean one."

G.C. pushed a button under the table and its legs began to fold. The table sank slowly to the floor, hitting Clarence on the shin. With a yelp, he began hopping up and down, going around and around as if he were doing a dance.

Mrs. Philpott grabbed Freeman by the arm. "This isn't funny, young man."

"Yes mam." He hadn't realized that he had been standing there smiling, rather helplessly, since Clarence wrestled the plate from him. "It isn't funny."

The seventh and eighth grades had entered and taken their places quietly, looking on with a mixture of distaste, amusement and admiration. The fourth and fifth grades had left the cafeteria. The Special Education class, a non-graded group of retarded students, remained at their table, waiting for their teacher to return from the telephone call he usually made while they were eating. The sixth-grade girls sat at another table, disowning any association with this section of the class.

Mrs. Philpott suddenly discovered the stray Birdie Powell and ordered, "You get to wherever you belong." To the rest of them, "Now we'll sit down right here until the matter is cleared up."

The sat on the benches with the table between them like a fallen warrior. "First of all, as I've said a hundred times, the cafeteria is for eating."

Billy dug an elbow into Freeman's ribs. "Anybody can eat it can have it."

"What's this?" Silence. "When I want humor, I'll hire you as a comic, Billy Blackburn. Now, there will be no talking. Who started this disturbance?" Silence. "I'm asking a question. Why am I getting no answers?"

G.C. raised his hand. "You said no talking."

"I very well know what I said, and I meant the kind of ad-libbing you're doing. Now I want an answer to my question." Silence. "Very well, the entire table will be punished."

"Kick it," Billy said to Freeman. When Freeman ignored the suggestion, he said to G.C., "Let's punish it."

They eased their toes under the table, then kicked.

"What's going on here?" Mrs. Philpott took a long audible breath. "Straight line, no talking, and march to your room, without drinks, without restroom privileges, and without afternoon recess. If you can't act better, then I'll have to treat you worse. Get out health books, and we'll see what we can learn about nutrition and about table manners. And I don't want a word spoken before I get there."

She went to the teachers' table to collect her purse and a small booklet.

"Peas and raisins," Clarence said at the end of the line.

"I said there would be no talking. Wait and walk with me."

Clarence slowed to fall in step with Mrs. Philpott. "I was talking to you. It's the peas and raisins all the time. They ought to know we don't like 'em by the size of the garbage."

"Maybe they don't measure the garbage. Peas and raisins are healthful and economical."

Freeman had heard her say to another teacher, "Somebody must have a friend who owns a pea patch. Four times in two weeks and these students never eat them."

Back in the classroom, Mrs. Philpott's eyes searched each face, as if expecting to find the answers to her questions written there. Freeman opened his book and kept his eyes on it without seeing a word.

Mom, if he told her, which he probably wouldn't unless she first heard it somewhere else, would not like the total-class punishment for the disturbance Billy had started. Mom hadn't been as happy with the new consolidated school, which had taken in all the one-, two- and three-room schools in the area, as she might have been if the school board hadn't forced her to sell the land to them. It was her best piece of land and she hadn't really wanted to sell it at all.

"I wanted to save that for Freeman. He could build him a house and have all the lawn and garden he'd ever need and be close by all the time," she'd said when they offered her eighteen thousand dollars for it. When she insisted it was not for sale, Mr. Prater, the board member who'd come to talk with her about it, had told her they would condemn it and take it away, for it was the best site for the school. "You name the price," he'd encouraged. Then Mom had told him it was worth twice what he'd offered, pieces of level land which were dry and flood-free being as scarce as they were. "Name a price," he'd repeated. And Mom had said, "The least I'd think about would be twenty-five thousand." Without consulting Mom further, they had taken the case to court. Freeman remembered how softly and slowly Prater had said that day, "The court's condemned the property for eighteen thousand." And how there had been a bitterness he still did not understand in Mom's voice when she said, "Courts can do anything they like. It still doesn't always turn out best. Might doesn't prove right."

Building of the new school had started that summer. At about the same time, the Highway Department had begun extending the blacktop road up Toms Creek for ten miles. It had been a busy autumn, with trucks hauling supplies and asphalt sixteen hours a day.

"Getting more like New York every day," Pop

55

said when a diesel truck roared through the night, disturbing their sleep and spewing a black stench through the little valley that forced them to close the windows and turn on fans.

"I'd rather have my peace and quiet," Mom said. "Bring in strangers and disturb the land and—oh, everything. Wish I'd been one of the early settlers. We don't need the money badly enough to see the land torn up and the air polluted as it is. We had enough to do us."

"Then you could give the money back," Pop said in his teasing voice.

"If I could trade back, I'd trade this minute. If I could trade all the way back to those settlers who let the companies come in and fleece them, I'd do it. No wonder we've all grown up with a fear of strangers, especially dressed-up strangers. And that some people are afraid to let their children get much education. The men who robbed them did it with educated words, by mouth and paper, and they'd not choose their children to learn to scheme in such a manner."

"I feel the same way, Viney," Pop said. "But we can't change it and we can't stop it."

For a while they sat on the back porch during the summer evenings, hoping to get away from the dust and smoke and noise. Then they praised the "old days" when they sold cattle and groceries and crops and Pop walked five miles to get to his job with the Highway Department, which was building roads far away.

"Your mom's folks settled this valley," Pop said one evening as they watched the black trail of diesel-oil fumes drifting toward them. "Tom Varney was wise when he said, 'Land don't grow and I feel it my bounded duty to take as much of it as possible off the hands of them that don't love it and won't take care of it.' Your mom's seen this place grow from near wilderness with only a bridle path. When they get that cut through to Boldmans Branch and Toler, get the big school done, and the railroad through, it'll never be the same. Like moving a hundred years in four or five."

Now those projects were finished. And Mom had said only a week or so ago, "Does progress have to be so ugly and noisy and dangerous?"

"I don't think it has to, but it is," Pop had answered. "Progress! People away from here've worried about our lack of progress. I don't think we've gained enough to ever pay for our loss of privacy. Twenty-five cents an acre they got for mineral rights, wasn't it, Viney?"

"Even Pa got fooled into thinking he could have his cake and eat it too. He took the money he got for what few rights he sold and bought more land. But he never dreamed they'd have them big dozers and shovels and trucks and augers taking over. Thought they'd just open little coal banks, like people had then, and gouge around with picks and shovels and ponies. Nobody then ever dreamed they'd scalp the mountains and leave them to slide into the creeks. But since we can't do a thing about it now, we'd as well talk about something pleasant. That wild honeysuckle's like living in a perfume bottle. Smell that. And I love hearing the bees and seeing the birds swarming after it."

Freeman's attention suddenly returned to the classroom as he realized that Mrs. Philpott was walking back and forth with a pale kind of sternness. When her back was turned, he whispered to Clarence, two seats in front of him, "Where's my dogs?"

"Catching groundhogs. Got two last night. Going again tonight. Had groundhog and gravy for breakfast." Clarence kept a pencil on the book. "You want to start something?"

They really weren't Freeman's dogs. He had never laid claim to them, but he played with them and fed them and sometimes went walking with them just to watch them sniff and paw the ground. He knew this wasn't the proper time or place to pick at Clarence, but he was tired of always taking smart remarks and sly grins. "Mom said you could keep them."

"Cheaper to borrow. And what she wants and what she gets can be a horse of another color."

"What's that supposed to mean?"

"That's for me to know and you to find out. You don't know your elbow from a hole in the ground."

Mrs. Philpott snapped her fingers. "If I hear another word from back there, some boys are going to get a week's detention. Buddies should hold their secrets until after school."

Surely Mrs. Philpott knew that they weren't buddies. If Freeman had a buddy, it was Birdie Powell. They had been in every grade together until this year. Clarence acted more like an enemy than a friend. Why? He hadn't done anything to Clarence. He decided to stop Clarence in the hallway after school and demand to know why Clarence was such a smart aleck with him. Clarence was sharp-tongued with everybody, defending himself before there was a need for defense, throwing out reasons for starting a fight—and he could fight, never giving up even when he was whipped once by Billy and G.C. —but it seemed to Freeman that he was doubly mean to him.

5

The lost letter became important again as Freeman walked home. He could hear Pop cutting grass in the back yard and Mom in the kitchen rattling pans as he tiptoed upstairs and began looking for it. He slammed a drawer mainly for the release slamming a drawer could give to his disappointment and also to see what Mom might say.

"If Chicken Licken were to hear that, she'd swear the sky was falling. Is that you, Freeman?"

"Me, me, me, me," he said as if he were singing. "I'm looking for a piece of paper that got misplaced."

"Want French fries for supper?"

He ignored the question. "I'm looking for a letter from Billy's aunt, Willie something-or-other." When Mom failed to answer, he called loudly as he came down the stairs, "I'm looking for a letter. I left it on my bed last night, and it disappeared. It was to Aunt Mag." He stood facing her, but she kept her eyes on the knife she was using to slice potatoes. "Mom?" She went to the refrigerator for a cabbage and began trimming the outer leaves and letting them drop into the sink. "Mom, if you got that letter, you give it back to me. It's Aunt Mag's."

"Had a big chunk of potato in my mouth and was trying to be polite and not speak," she explained. "I meant to mention it this morning but it slipped my mind. I went up to see if your window was closed. The wind had blown a piece of paper to the hallway and I picked it up and stuck it in my apron pocket and forgot all about it till I started getting ready for bed. Saw then it was a letter to Mag and couldn't imagine how it got there."

"Billy gave it to me," Freeman said.

"Mag was down here a few minutes yesterday, but I didn't think she went upstairs. Then I thought maybe she went up to the bathroom while I fixed us some coffee. I called her this morning and she came down and got it, but she didn't remember having it with her yesterday. I'm sorry you got upset about it. But I can't imagine why Billy'd be carrying his grandma's letter around and why you'd have it."

Pop came in from cutting the grass. "Hamburger, mmm. Mom sure does know how to feed hungry men, doesn't she?"

Freeman was still thinking about the letter and didn't answer.

Pop washed his hands at the sink. "What's wrong? Cat got your tongue? Something bad happen at school, like a low grade?"

Freeman shook his head.

"Could you sweep the grass off the walks, son?" Mom asked.

Freeman took the broom and went out, waiting just outside the door to see if either of them spoke about the letter. He heard the TV being tuned, heard Mom turn on water. After sweeping the walk, he attacked some dandelions nestling so close to the ground that the mower had missed them, small golden clusters as pretty as any of Mom's flowers. But she liked her flowers in clumps or rows along the walks and around the edge of the yard, not sprinkled over it as these were. He dug up a worm and squatted to see if he had injured it and was glad he had not. He had just missed a good opportunity to ask some questions. Starting with the letter. Maybe beginning with Pop's wanting to know why he was so quiet. He always took the easy way out. Old Easy-Going Freeman. He was old enough to hear about what had happened to his father and mother, no matter what it had been.

Maybe Billy had only wanted to disturb him. Maybe Billy knew he was happy and wanted to upset him. But could he hide away forever in a snug little cocoon? No, it was time, time to force things into the open. He would stop being so quiet and easily satisfied and ask some questions.

He was still on his knees with the worm when Pop called, "Fixing to dig a swimming pool, son?"

Freeman turned the worm over and saw that he had reached a passageway of some kind. "Pop, look. What is this?"

"Mole tunnel, I guess. There's a whole world beneath the one we see and hear. Mom's fixing that good fruit salad with nuts. Here, let me help you fill in the holes a little. I'll rake the dirt in and you step on it and tamp it in."

Mom was chopping nuts. "Why don't you go and drive Old Nell down from the pasture. It's getting late so don't poke now."

Pop groaned. "My lunch's settled to the bottom of my big toe. Plenty of time later. We could eat first, couldn't we?"

"Be a while before it's ready," Mom said.

Freeman liked going to the pasture. He crossed the creek and climbed the gate. A swarm of gnats circled his head and he kept waving them away. In the distance, a stand of tall slender poplars looked clean and almost bare, the few yellow and brown leaves quivering although there was no breeze. Around him, goldenrod stood erect, a beautiful sun color, with each tiny blossom perfectly formed on each of the fingerlike parts of the whole flower. A woolly worm crossed a log and detoured around a crow pecking on the ground. The crow scolded and took off, its blue-black wings fanning Freeman's hair.

On the flat above the house, he called, "Nell, you old skinflint. Nell, where are you hiding?" He looked over the slopes and the hollows, then past the shallow creek that flooded the backside of the bottoms each spring, past the garden with its brown cornstalks leaning in every direction and the dark green cabbage stalks. From this height the yard was a green carpet with touches of brown, like a tweed design. The house was a toy, with coal dust streaking the green shingles. Mom came to the midget-sized green door, shaded by the porch and by hollyhocks, and shook a dust mop in quick jerks. She looked like a doll-sized puppet.

He found Old Nell drinking at a spring near the top of the hill. She rolled her eyes and flicked her ears as if asking why he was interrupting her privacy. "You go on now, will you? Go on." He patted her, gave her a little slap, then threw a stone so that it rolled along beside her.

When she started down the hill, he sat down. She would go slowly, picking a bite of grass here and there. He scratched his name on a big white rock with a bit of yellow rock he found near it, wrote initials and thought how nice the world really was when you could look at it from a distance. How easy it was to forget any problems and feel free and peaceful up here. It got crowded when people were around. He didn't always understand why they did what they did, and they didn't understand him. He was alone here, but not lonely. Not lonely as he had been a few times when he daydreamed that he had brothers and sisters: the brothers would be ball players, the sisters pigtailed and freckled, following the boys, wanting to play ball. He could imagine brothers and sisters easily. A father and mother came harder. He had tried to invent them, but they never quite fitted his needs, for they always went away. Sometimes they left with a circus. Once they were missionaries in a heathen land. Once they were in a hospital with a contagious disease. The circus was better, for circuses came home at the end of a season.

Maybe they were auctioneers. It would be an active and exciting life to travel about selling things. When the school board won the land at court for the consolidated school, the old school building had been auctioned off to the highest bidder. Freeman had had a cold and couldn't go out in the drizzly weather, but he could hear the auctioneer's chant from where he sat on the back porch: "Got eighteen, eighteen, eighteen. Who'll make it nineteen, who'll make it twenty, twenty, twenty, who'll make it twenty, nineteen I got, who'll make it nineteen and a half?"

He'd been shelling peas for Mom to put in the freezer, and he'd imagined himself buying the old building for twenty-five dollars and moving into it. He would let cobwebs grow until they hung like moss from trees he'd seen in pictures of the south. The eaves would become crowded with nests— wrens, wasps, hornets, mud daubers and mice. Ants would crawl over his table and mosquitoes and moths would fly about his oil lamp. He would always leave the door open so that any animal needing a home could come and go whenever it wanted. Some day, after he got tired of living in the school house, he would go off in a plane or a train to a desert for a short while, then he'd go to the ocean. And he'd be boss. He'd be so right no one would ever tell him he was wrong.

The hamburgers and French fries should be ready. There was an exact moment for eating them if they were at their best, just as there was an exact moment for nearly everything. Old Nell stopped a few yards down the hill and waited. He got up and stood looking far away, up the hollow where Aunt Mag lived. Three hills came together, layer on layer, like leaves on a tree. There was a giant yellow blob, like a bug, climbing one of the hills. Only it wasn't a bug: trees were falling before it, toppling over slowly, and behind it was a yellowish path. A bull-dozer making a road. Maybe opening a coal seam, or getting ready to open one.

Freeman broke a great stalk of ironweed and flapped Old Nell's tail to get her started. A milkweed pod burst before his eyes and the tiny silken parachutes with seeds on them began floating about. He found a stalk with the pods still closed. With some varnish on them, to glue the seams together, milkweed pods made pretty decorations. The royal purple blossoms of the ironweed would look nice in the milk-glass vase on the living room mantel. If Mom didn't want it, he'd take it to Mrs. Philpott.

"Freeman?" Pop called at the foot of the hill. "What's the rush?"

"The man'll be here any minute now."

A chill swept over Freeman, as if a wind had started to blow and him with no coat. He began to run toward Pop. He didn't have to ask what man. It was Bob Phillips. They had mentioned him last night. Phillips came through Toms Creek with a truck once a month, regular as a clock, and he bought whatever livestock was for sale. He was a short fat man who pretended to be going out of business with each purchase. He had bought a pig from them last year.

"You're not selling Old Nell? You can't!" he shouted.

"She's getting frail, son. That horse's getting old. We can get what little plowing we need done with Daniel's machine, and you hardly ever ride her anymore."

"Why didn't you tell me? Why didn't you ask me?"

"We've been trying to. I thought you understood. I guess you just weren't listening."

A gray-green truck stopped. Bob Phillips got out of it and started toward them, a pleased smile on his face.

Freeman could only think that they hadn't really told him, hadn't really asked him, that they'd tricked him into driving Old Nell down to have her ready for Phillips. They thought he was a child and didn't matter!

He wanted to hurt them as they had hurt him. "Sell her and I'll leave! When you don't need me any longer, I guess you'll get rid of me too." The words came out as if they were steam exploding. He started running toward the house. "And never mention me again, like my daddy and mother!"

Mom was a small, humped blur standing at the lower end of the barn lot, leaning on the empty pig pen. Pop was shaking hands with Phillips. Maybe they were too shocked to answer him. Maybe they wanted to pretend, in front of Phillips, that he hadn't spoken. He threw the ironweed stalk and the milkweed pod on the table and went through the house so quickly the smell of food did not reach him until he was at the top of the stairs. He shut the door of his room and threw himself across the bed.

If they sold Old Nell, he *would* leave. He would go, first of all, to Aunt Mag's and ask for the true story. Maybe he'd only get one side of the truth, but it would be more than he now had. Aunt Mag liked talking and knew everything that had ever happened in the family. Then what would he do? He would figure that out later. Maybe he could go to an orphans' home.

Sobs shook him. At first, he tried to stop them. He pounded his fists on the mattress until his arms grew tired. After a while the tears stopped, but his body continued to heave for a long time.

6

Freeman heard them return to the house a few minutes after Phillips's truck left. He heard Mom say, "Think I should call him to supper?" Pop answered, "He knows supper's ready. Let him eat when he gets ready."

He took a book from the head of the bed and began reading. Reading always helped him to forget himself, but the picnic the boys were having in the story didn't help Freeman's hunger. As he grew hungrier, he grew noisier. But they didn't seem to hear when he squeaked the bed or moved a chair. He was determined that he was not going to eat unless they called him. His stomach growled. Finally, he decided to sneak down and get something. From the top of the stairs, he could tell they were still in the kitchen. They must have thought he was in his room with the door closed, because they were talking about him. "We've spoiled him, and we swore we wouldn't," Pop said.

Mom said, "He's big enough to know it's supper-time."

Pop said, "Maybe we should have told him a lot of things long ago. It's hard to even think about explaining, and the longer we wait the harder it's getting, Viney."

When he heard them get up from the table, he tiptoed back a few feet and stood waiting. Maybe it wasn't proper for him to eavesdrop, but it was one way of hearing what might not be said otherwise. What about the horse, he wanted to shout. Say something about Old Nell. They didn't. When they started to come upstairs, he went back to his room and closed the door. Maybe they expected him to come out and apologize. But he wouldn't, not ever, if they'd sold Old Nell.

He tried to imagine himself staying in the room day after day and meal after meal until he starved to death. A martyr. It was an exciting thought for a minute, but he knew, in reality, it would be horribly impossible. He liked eating and Mom was a good cook. They would be going to Centerville tomorrow for some shopping. They would get up at the usual time, get ready early and leave. Early birds got the parking spaces. Early birds got finished early. Wait a minute! There were some cookies in his dresser. He ate a half dozen cookies, got crumbs in the bed, had to get out and shake the covers. He expected to lie awake for hours, but he fell asleep almost immediately.

The next morning Mom called him to set the table. "We didn't sell Old Nell," she said to the top of his head. When he looked up, she continued, "Because we gave in, doesn't mean everytime you want something you can take a tantrum and get it, Freeman. We're going to figure on you taking care of her. She's going to need that corn chopped up."

"Gee thanks. Thanks, Mom, that's great."

He wanted to throw his arms about her, to bury his head in her arms. But sometimes he felt as if there were a glass wall between them. They could see each other, most of the time, and hear each other, but they couldn't see all or hear all, and they couldn't quite touch each other.

"Don't take up too much with that dog," she had said once when he was romping with a puppy he had found whimpering at the kitchen door. She had agreed he could keep the dog, if no one claimed it, but she also warned, "He'll run off and get lost or run over or something. Then you'll be hurt, son." One day the dog did disappear, but Freeman had had a great year with him.

Mom was too afraid he would be hurt. She was standing between him and every danger she could foresee. "I'd rather stay on an even keel myself," she'd said once. "I don't get over things as easily as maybe I should."

72

Freeman wondered if maybe she kept herself from touching him very often because she was afraid he would disappear. Standing beside her at the table, where she was placing fluffy homemade biscuits on a plate, he was surprised to find she was so small. He was at least an inch taller! And she had always seemed a giant to him.

He patted her on the shoulder. "Mom, you're shrinking or I'm stretching, one. Look here."

"Maybe a little of both." She turned to the stove for hot blackberry jam and spooned it over the butter on the saucer beside his plate.

When Pop came in, she kept her back to the table, busily wiping grease spatters from the stove. Pop said, "I guess Mom told you we didn't sell the horse. We didn't know she meant that much to you. Seems you don't pay her much mind any more. And she's old, Freeman, a lot older than most horses are. She was what you might call middle-aged when we bought her, before you were born. She wasn't a saddle horse, just a plain work horse, but you took up with her. Well, if you want her, it's your job to take care of her, your job entirely."

Freeman opened his mouth to promise that he'd take care of Old Nell, but at that minute Mom said, "Isn't this a nice day? Time we were getting ready for our shopping, soon as you boys get set to go."

After their being so good about the horse, maybe he should go with them, but he had decided before getting out of bed that he wouldn't go, that he'd stay home and just loaf around. "If you don't mind, I'll not go today," he said.

"You still feeling bad about the horse?" Pop asked.

"No, I feel fine. Glad. Anything you want me to do?"

Pop examined his shirt collar to see that it was behaving properly. "Nothing special that I know of. What's on your mind?"

"Nothing." It was true. Staying home just seemed more interesting and more independent than going to Centerville and back.

"You're sure it's not because you feel sick or anything?" Freeman nodded to Mom's question. "You won't go over there around the coal dock?" He shook his head. "And you won't play with a knife or anything dangerous?"

"I'm not a baby, Mom. No."

Pop took up the examination. "You're not planning on going anywhere?"

"I hadn't planned to."

Pop sounded a little reluctant. "Well, I guess it'll be all right." Then more cheerfully, "Want us to get anything?"

They said good-by and reminded him again to be careful. Mom thought of two or three extra things she needed to do. Freeman wanted to rush them off, but when they were gone, he felt lonely. He picked up the telephone, but it was out of order. Some phone on their party line must have been left off the hook. He turned on the TV and turned it off. He picked up a puzzle and laid it down. He went to the barn and gave Old Nell some small ears of corn, propped the pasture gate back so the prop would not be in her way and set out a new salt brick for her.

He couldn't explore the deserted coal dock or whittle or examine the gun because he had promised. If he hadn't promised, he might not have thought of these things, but the fact that he couldn't do them suddenly made him feel as if he were fenced in. Back at the house, he made a toasted cheese sandwich. He wasn't hungry, but Mom hadn't said he couldn't use the toaster. Whenever she was going to be out of his sight for even a few minutes she used to warn him not to light the gas and not to use the toaster. Maybe she was giving him more freedom because she thought he was growing up. He made a layer of dill pickles and of sweet peppers on the sandwich and went to lie in the front porch swing.

"Yoohoo," Birdie called. "How come you didn't go with them?"

"Just didn't." Birdie was in the yard now. Freeman invited him to share the sandwich and the swing. Birdie came to the store about once a week, but he usually didn't have time for visiting.

"Boy, you've sure got it made in the shade," Birdie said.

"You think so?'" Maybe that was one reason Freeman liked Birdie so much; instead of making him shrink as Billy and Clarence tried to do, Birdie gave him reason for expanding, made him stretch like a pleased cat, made him feel important.

"I know so. Your own room and all." Birdie shared a room with four brothers, and he thought a separate room was like having a special good fairy all your own.

"It's not all that grand." Maybe Birdie wanted to see the room; he hadn't been up there since they'd redecorated it in the spring. "Want to go up? I've got some new records."

"Another time, huh? I thought you might go down to Uncle Ike's cane mill with me. They're going to finish making molasses today. You stay up in this neck of the woods and never know what's going on down the way. A path to the schoolhouse and back."

"Oh, I have a lot of things to do and they like me to stay close."

"You're weaned, I reckon. We could rush back and not let them know you went off. Did you promise not to go out?" Birdie blew a bubble and popped it. "Boy, you make a mean sandwich."

Every time Freeman saw him that wad of gum seemed to have grown. Maybe Birdie never discarded any of it. He led the way to the kitchen and made another sandwich for Birdie. He hadn't said he wouldn't go anywhere. He had said he hadn't planned to. That should take care of it. Anyone could change plans.

He set out mustard, mayonnaise and catsup for Birdie. "Wish you lived a little closer."

"I'll put in an order that the next time we move it'll be closer to Freeman Sloan, all right?" He walked and ate his way to the back porch. "A mile I hoofed it up here to see you, bud. Of course, Mommy wanted some beans, if you had any in the store, and I didn't tell her I saw your folks go out to town. She said I could stay at the mill awhile. Apron strings or not, you can't complain with all you've got. Still, I wish they'd let you come down and loaf with me and stay all night. Have to hang you up on a nail, us not having another inch of room in a bed." Birdie grinned, and two big freckles on the right side of his cheek came together and made one large brown patch the color of his hair. "Your bike in operation?"

Freeman's bicycle was on the smokehouse porch. He remembered Mom had said they once lived in the smokehouse. It was about the size of Abraham Lincoln's cabin. When they gave him the bicycle at

Christmas, they had laid down one rule: Never ride on the highway. That was long ago, and maybe they wouldn't mind now. He took off the piece of plastic covering it.

"Boy, that's neat." Birdie stepped back to admire it. "If you think they won't care, we can double down."

"They might."

"Then let's not stir up two hornets' nests. Just going down there'll be fun enough." Birdie started toward the highway.

Freeman followed. "They get mad, they can scratch their mad place." He had heard Billy say that about his grandmother, with a carefree air that had made him seem a man of his own. Somehow when Freeman said it, it didn't quite come off. He was sorry immediately. He didn't have to play tough with Birdie.

"You know something?" Freeman said.

"Maybe one thing, but not enough to hurt anybody to carry it."

"I don't have to do any big-talk with you. We don't even have to talk when we're together."

"Timber!" a voice shouted before they'd gone a quarter mile.

"Clarence up there making mining posts," Birdie said. "He helps his dad every Saturday and gets paid a dollar." A small log came sliding down the hill to join three others which had stopped in the culvert at the ditch line. "Wish I could make me some money." Birdie put his arm around Freeman's shoulder and shook him playfully. "Old moneybags here doesn't have to worry about minor expenses."

"Woodenhead," Clarence said to someone with him.

A voice answered Clarence, "You've got a splinter on the brain."

"That's Goober,'" Birdie said. "Bet he's come to stay awhile at Bill Jack's. You ever think how many kids on this creek live with their grandparents?" When Freeman shook his head, Birdie dropped behind to follow the narrow, dry path on the edge of the road. "Them trucks are tearing up the pea patch with this road. Ground the blacktop right into the ground." He broke a birch twig leaning over the road and offered a piece to Freeman. "Doesn't taste as good as in the spring when the sap's up."

Clarence shouted down, "You guys better get out'n the way! One of these posts'll rip right through you, guts and all."

"Hey, need any help? What's this job pay?" Birdie called.

"Nickel's worth of five-dollar bills. Where you jaspers headed to?" Clarence held onto a small poplar and leaned over the cliff. "Freeman, in the flesh. Done flew the coop?"

Another voice, that of Bill Jack, scolded, "You hush that right now." Lower, "Pick on him all the time." Louder, "Why don't you fellows come up and join us, see how working men get the salt goes in their bread?" To someone with him, in a lower voice, "Brute that log over a little. Then trim off that snag."

A power saw started. Birdie tossed a rock at a clump of willows and a pheasant flew out. The bird nodded its head, then went back into the shelter.

The sweet smell of boiling cane juice reached them before they were at the mill. They broke stalks from a stacked pile of cane and joined the circle around the upper end of the pan. Dip, lick, dip, lick. Freeman couldn't decide which was better, the steam rolling back, with a slight breeze, into his face or the taste of the warm golden foam. They stood beside the pan for a while and chased the foam rising from the center of the upper frame, barely letting it cool before popping it into their mouths.

Ike Caines, known as Uncle Ike to everyone out of respect for his age, was seated in a homemade rocking chair and whittling paddles for visitors. His long white beard stirred lightly with the breeze and parted on the unbuttoned front of his blue chambray shirt. Aunt Rhoda stood beside him telling who was who. Although she was Uncle Ike's

second wife, and a good thirty years younger, Freeman couldn't help thinking she was the one in the
old song, and he hummed softly, "Go tell Aunt
Rhody the old gray goose is dead." She pushed back
the black sunbonnet, took up the tail of a great white
apron and wiped her eyes. She motioned Freeman
and Birdie over and gave them paddles.

She sat down on a stool someone handed her and
studied Freeman briefly. "Let's see now. You look
like somebody I know."

"I'm Freeman Sloan."

"My goodness, and you grown up. Last time I
saw you, you was knee high to a grasshopper. Uncle
Ike," she said to her husband, "this is George and
Viney Sloan's grandchild. Remember Viney Varney
married George Sloan from over Toler way?"

"Howdy." Uncle Ike lifted a gallus strap with the
end of the knife, then wiped the knife on his black
serge pants.

"Don't. You'll hurt yourself," she scolded.

He stared at her as if she were a sassy child. "Girl,
I've been using a knife since before you's born, and
I've never cut a thing yet I didn't mean to cut."

She patted him gently. "That's not saying you
never will."

He slapped at a yellowjacket with the new paddle
he'd begun. "Remember like it was today the day
your daddy and mother got married, indeed I do."

Aunt Rhoda stooped so that her face was directly before his and said, "Want me to get you another piece of wood?"

"Need a new knife. Been a coon's age since I skinned anybody in a knife-swapping."

She motioned and a man came to talk knives with Uncle Ike. The boys went back to eating molasses. Freeman looked at the far end of the pan, where a man was scooping the scummy top from the juice and dumping it into a hole.

"Time to pay for your bait of sorghums now," the man said.

They fed some cane through the grinder, carried two pails of freshly ground juice and poured it into the lower end of the pan. Then they stacked an armload of dry wood beside the low grate under the pan before going to jump on the warm damp pile of discarded cane stalks.

"Whoo-hoo, look what's turned loose on us now. Just saw the family carriage go up the road. Now I know why they drove so fast."

Billy and G.C. were headed toward them.

"Want to straighten this out for good?" Birdie asked.

"Nah," Freeman said. "I better get home."

They ignored the boys and started across the field toward the highway.

"Scared?" G.C. shouted. "Fraidy cat, fraidy cat's

afraid of her shadow and all that! How about it? Run, run, the way cats've always done!"

"Don't let that past the outer ear," Birdie said.

"Aw, we didn't want to get tied up with you," Billy called. "Just keeping my growl in practice. And wanted to tell you a secret, but I guess I better not. Swore to Grandma I wouldn't tell a living soul."

"Tell him then," G.C. said. "Him and his pal's both deadheads. Oh all right, let's go eat that pan of 'lasses and pay no mind to a bunch of roadrunners."

Billy and G.C. had left their bicycles at a sign which read Parking For All Vehicles. Billy propped his foot on a ridge of dirt, as if daring Birdie and Freeman to come back.

"Saving his bicycle?" G.C. said. "That's the way to have things, my mom always tells me. 'You get something,' she says, 'and you want to wear it out. Now you take that Freeman Sloan, why he takes care of his bike. Shoe leather's a lot cheaper.'"

Freeman and Birdie walked away and left G.C. talking.

"Want me to go a ways with you?" Birdie asked.

"Nah, their bark's worse than their bite. That G.C.'s so lazy if he was a dog he wouldn't scratch a flea."

"We're going to have to figure out what's bugging those guys. See you Monday."

Freeman watched to see if Billy and G.C. were

going to follow. When they appeared busy eating molasses, he was still not certain they might not take after him, and he kept walking faster until he was running. Clarence was in the ditch, driving a wedge into a post. Freeman planned to say "hi" without stopping, but Clarence saw him coming.

"Lordy, but you're in a rash of a hurry. What's after you, old pal, old buddy?" Clarence stood leaning against the sledge hammer, one foot still propped on the post.

Freeman panted, "Getting my exercise."

"Well, law-de-daw, it's nice there's people in the world so well padded they can run for exercise."

Freeman kept on running.

"Clarence? Clarence!" Bill Jack roared. "Stop fooling around down there and get to work."

Freeman's stomach churned as he ran. Up, down, up, down, up, up, up. He was sick. He shouldn't have eaten so much. He wished he'd stayed home. Why hadn't he gone with Mom and Pop? Would they be mad? Why couldn't he ever do anything right?

7

Pop was standing with an elbow on the rail fence at the lower side of the barn, looking toward the hill. He looked up when Freeman came scooting down the steep slope.

"You had us worried, son. Where've you been?"

"Down to Uncle Ike's cane mill. You didn't say I had to stay here. I didn't mean to be gone so long." Pop's face kept that long, faraway look. "What's the matter? Pop, what's wrong?"

"You fed the horse?"

Freeman nodded, but Pop wasn't looking at him. "Yes, sir, I fed her some small stuff, some little bitty nubbins."

"Oh." Pop's breath came out and stopped, like a teacher giving a phonics lesson. "Old Nell's dead. Choked on that corn. Maybe if you hadn't gone off, you'd a heard her and got help. Maybe not. It's too late to know."

Freeman looked away from Pop and toward the house. Mom was standing at the gate, still wearing her good dress and with a puzzled look on her face. Whatever argument he might use in defense of his actions didn't seem worthwhile. He opened his mouth and his voice was only a small croak. Saying he was sorry wouldn't help anything. It was too late to help Old Nell. He wanted to run and hide. To shout angrily. To cry out that it wasn't true. And doing any of this, or all of it, wouldn't change the situation.

Mom unbuttoned the lace collar of her dress. "Thought you said you were staying here."

Whatever they wanted to say or do, he deserved it. Freeman stood there waiting for blame to be heaped on him, welcoming it.

Pop loosened his hold on the fence and said, "It might've happened and us all here." He walked to the upper corner of the lot, pulled a jimson weed and tossed it onto the truck road.

Mom set up a quick lunch of canned soup, sandwiches and leftover pie, for which they had little appetite. She talked a little about Old Nell: about how the horse had never jumped a fence and had never bitten anyone or tried to kick. Freeman felt sadder and sadder. That they were not shouting "you're to blame" did not take away his feeling of guilt. If only they would shout sometime about something, it seemed to him that the unseen walls might be broken down. If they could say what they thought, if they would defend their own positions on anything heartily and heatedly instead of being smooth as a pool of rain water.

Every once in a while Pop said, "Let's not blame anybody. It could've happened on chopped corn, on cornmeal, and us all here."

"Still," Mom said, "we left with a false impression—that you weren't going off—and don't try to scrouge around with words and find loopholes out of that."

Freeman wanted to protest that he was old enough to make a few decisions, that he wanted to make some decisions, that he needed to make some, even if he made a few mistakes in doing so. But this was not the proper time for it. The decision he'd made today had turned out so badly he couldn't defend it, even silently. It might've happened *if* he'd stayed home, *if* he'd chopped the corn, *if* he'd never left the barn. But the *if* was there. After the big disturbance last night over the horse. After the happiness this morning.

"This is awful, losing her," he said.

"Everybody loses at times. It's hard to accept and hard to live with. Some people seem to take loss easier than others. I guess your mom and I are sorry losers. There's a proper balance somewhere, and we're still looking for it," Pop said.

"And maybe we've been shirking some other re-

sponsibilities. Maybe we've been good at that, too."
Mom was up now, rinsing her glass, raking her half-
eaten sandwich onto a plate for the dogs. "What're
we going to do, George? People burn dead horses,
don't they?"

The very idea made Freeman sick. All the day's
troubles were his, and he made no effort to control
his temper. "You worried about that twenty-five dollars you lost? I'll pay you back! I'll pay you for every
cent you've ever spent on me, ever lost on account
of me. And you'll not burn my horse!"

He stumbled blindly over a rug on the end of the
porch and would have fallen had he not slammed
into a post which nearly winded him. He sat down.
The freezer, on the end of the porch near the door,
was running, running, and the sound seemed to
bore into him. He leaped up and ran to the smokehouse. He wanted to jump on his bike and start
riding. But that wouldn't help. He'd have to return
and the horse would be there. He got a shovel and
started toward the barn.

"Freeman, wait," Pop called. "Come here a minute. Let's sit down and think this thing through
sensibly."

They sat on the edge of the porch. "No need for
you to feel mad at anybody, and certainly not at us."
Pop scraped at some paint flakes on the floor. "Nobody we can hire with a pick and shovel, and we

couldn't dig a hole big enough in a week. She can't be dumped out somewhere. It's against the law, and we'd not be able to haul her in the pickup anyway. What do you think?"

"We won't burn her!"

"Then you tell me what we'll do." When Mom came to the porch and cleared her throat, Pop said, "Viney, how about letting us iron this out? It was and still is his horse." Mom left. "No two ways about it, we've got a dead horse on our hands and a lot of work no matter what we decide. That's the reason we wanted to sell her. Thought it would be easier on you to see her go off alive. Maybe if it hadn't been for the money—us thinking about getting her off our hands and saving us the sadness and the work and all and getting paid for it. . . . Would you've wanted us to give her to Phillips?"

"I don't know. But I do wish you'd told me."

"We tried, son. At least we tried to lead up to it, what you might call 'breaking it easy.' But it didn't work."

They really had, he remembered now. But they'd been breaking it too easy. He'd closed his ears and not tried to understand. Maybe "breaking things easy" was the way they thought things should be done, but it seemed to Freeman that once in a while things deserved to be taken a little hard. Maybe they'd been dropping a lot of hints about other things and he'd been too dense to understand or too involved with something else to pay attention. He wanted a whole package of facts, an entire history placed in a sentence or two. He wanted direct questions and answers and not what Aunt Mag would call "beating around the bush."

Pop broke into the silence with, "Well, starting right now, what're we going to do?"

Freeman wanted to recall the entire morning. And not have the slightest feeling that he might be blamed. He wanted to defend himself even when he knew Pop did not expect it and that it would not clear anything. He was always ready to defend himself, thinking he had a priority on that right. And he couldn't stand that very thing in others!

Mom picked up a rug at the door, shook it over the side of the porch, then returned to the kitchen.

"Could I go up and get Ben Harmon to come and doze a hole? He doesn't work at the mines on Saturdays. And I'll pay for it, Pop. I've got nearly a hundred dollars in the bank."

Mom took some cherries from the freezer. "Cherry pie for supper, boys. Cherry pie and ice cream."

Pop said, "You go on and get Ben Harmon, if that's the way you want it."

Ben Harmon dug the hole. Freeman watched that, but when the job of removing Old Nell from the stall to the hill came up, Pop said, "We've got a winch line and enough stuff here. You'd probably be in the way. Why don't you go out there and straighten around and sweep out the store? Mom's been complaining about its being so dusty."

Mom was standing at the kitchen door. When he got the key, she said, "Don't heave around anything heavy and hurt yourself now."

Where there had once been hundreds of combs, handkerchiefs and such small items hanging on the wall, there were only a few cardboard holders now. The bare nails were only brown lumps on the once-white walls. There was a smell of herbs, of ginseng, pennyroyal and lobelia, although no one had brought herbs to the store in the last four or five years.

Freeman swept out a corner, then moved some tools to it—a hoe, a rake, two brooms, a hammer and a mowing scythe. On the counter he made a pyramid with coffee cans, an igloo with sugar, hard as bricks in the bags. Mom and Pop had let their customers know that when the dry goods were gone they were not going to replace them, and fewer and fewer people were coming to the store. Before going out to open the store now, they asked a customer, "What do you want?" Mom had, only a few days before, enumerated things that would keep: "Soap, coffee, tissue paper, mops." Freeman piled empty boxes together and into them shoveled coal dust from the wall shelves and from the floor. Bubble gum, half a box. He stuck five pieces in his pocket and dropped a nickel into the box. He carried the trash down to the swamp and set fire to it. While it burned, he gathered up bits of material from other fires and tossed them into it.

"Not much left in there," he said when he went to the kitchen.

"Why don't you make us a right pretty 'Closed' sign and tack it on the door? Ten cents profit a day's not worth running back and forth." She found a piece of white cardboard from a shirt package and gave it to him.

At any other time, Freeman might have added a few curlicues to the letters or drawn a flower in the space at the end. He did not feel like decorating it today, so he left the letters plain and trimmed the edges of the paper. The sign was up when Pop returned.

On Monday morning, there was a stir of excitement at school.

"Pictures are in, the pictures are here," was the whisper.

The photographs which had been made the second day of school had arrived, but they would not be distributed until afternoon. "Give me one" and "I'll trade with you" went back and forth between friends. At two o'clock the folders of color prints were handed out. Lips pouted and groans rose. Freeman was disappointed, then fascinated, as were all the others.

"If you're going to raise a garden next year, put this on a stick and it'll substitute for a scarecrow," he told Birdie as they exchanged the small size.

"The spitting image of you, old boy. That mud dauber's nest could pass for me, too." Birdie's freckles did look bigger and browner and much more prominent than they did on his face, but it was a nice picture.

"Best trade I ever made." Freeman put the photograph in his billfold.

When he got home, he laid the folder on the end of the sink. Mom glanced at the eyes showing through the window of the folder. "Look like they're real plain." Then she went on with washing the window behind the sink.

The eagerness to share his likeness went down like a tire with a nail in it. Come to think of it, she never appeared very interested in photographs.

He pulled out the enlargement. "Think it's pretty?"

"Pretty is as pretty does." She had finished the window and was now scrubbing the bottom of a skillet with steel wool.

"It's not beautiful, for a fact."

Scrape. "Beauty's only skin deep." Scrape.

"Ugly as a mud fence."

"You're not. You're a fine-looking boy. You don't want me to get them messed up, do you? Lay them over there on the table."

"I gave Birdie one, but I can get it back if you don't want to pay for them."

"I never said anything about not paying for them, did I?"

"No, but we've got the house full of my pictures."

The invisible wall was between them again. Mom had closed him out. Freeman could see and hear her, but he could not touch her. They were not communicating at all.

She rinsed the pan and started scraping it again. "What do they do with the ones people don't take?"

"Burn them."

"We'll get us a frame and put the big one on the mantel."

"You don't have to."

"I said we'd take them. How much are they?" Rinse, scrape,

"Four dollars. And you never even looked. Because I said they'd be burned? If they went back to the company, the company'd burn them. Same difference."

"I guess you're right, but we're not that hard up.

94

Cut off one of the small ones for Pop and one for me and lay the rest of them in the top dresser drawer in your room."

There were at least a hundred pictures of Freeman, in the drawer, still in their folders. The enlarged ones had been framed each year and scattered around the house. Big deal, all that money tied up in old pictures that weren't worth a hill of beans to anybody.

Suddenly he realized that if she would spend four dollars rather than have his photographs burned, she would not have destroyed the pictures of his father, not unless she was a lot different then. She would have them somewhere, unless she had buried them. If they were buried, he would never find them; if they were not, he was going to locate them.

He counted off places they could not be—not in the smokehouse, not in the barn. His mind raced through the house, naming possible hiding places and discounting them. He went to the cellar and searched through two boxes. That left only the space between the roof and the ceiling. It wasn't really an attic, since there was no doorway and no stairs. It wasn't used for storage ordinarily. Hmmm. There was a hole in the ceiling of the bathroom closet, and shelves in the closet with bottles and jars and jugs on them. Why hadn't he thought of it before? If they caught him going up, they could find a good reason for stopping him. He would have to wait for a chance.

The opportunity came sooner than he had expected. After supper, Mom and Pop went to set out tulip bulbs.

Freeman excused himself with, "I should study." He smiled at his cleverness. He really should study, but he hadn't said that he was going to. For fear of being caught, he waited until Pop had a ridge half finished and Mom was on her knees planting bulbs. He stuck a flashlight in his pocket, moved enough things to have toe space and climbed into the blackest darkness he had ever seen. The light swept over emptiness until it reached the fourth corner. Under some old plastic curtains there were two boxes, one on the other. The top one had old clothes he had never seen. The larger box, with the word "Sauerkraut" written across its sides, had some damp-feeling papers and some trinkets—a piece of chain, a cheap costume ring, an empty red bottle. Freeman carried the large box to the opening. If he could get it to his room, he could hide it long enough to examine it all.

"Freeman, turn the water on there at the end of the house," Pop called, "and bring the hose here."

Freeman didn't want to loiter and be caught, and he didn't want to climb the steps again to bring the box down. Dropping it would make a noise they could hear. They'd think he had fallen and was hurt. He pushed aside bottles and threw down some paper towels and rolls of toilet tissue until there was room for the box on the top shelf. Then he began backing down the shelves as quickly as he could. He heard Mom say, "These don't have to have water. They don't come up till spring." Down another step. On the porch, Mom said, "You go up and see why Freeman didn't answer." Freeman eased the box to the floor. He had barely closed the closet door when Pop appeared.

"Thought you were studying."

"I'm going to." Freeman hurried to his room before Pop could notice the dust on his clothes. He made a loud noise of plopping himself at the table which served as his desk. He brushed off the dust and listened for Pop to leave the bathroom.

The telephone rang. Mom said, "Oh, it's you. . . . I don't think so. . . . I don't know. Talk to George. Telephone, George."

Pop said, "Really?" His voice lowered. "What brought this on? . . . We're all considerably older."

There were long silences between Pop's sentences, and he sounded as if he had to interrupt to get a word in. Freeman tiptoed out of his room, hoping to get the box to his room while they were busy.

"It was your decision, remember. We went along with it, then set up some rules of our own. . . . I'm sure you've known every move we've made. . . . You couldn't live under a rock cliff, and stop talking through your hat. . . . I don't know of anybody living under a cliff since the days when Indians had Jenny Wiley captured. . . . I guess we're all to blame. . . . Here."

This was too interesting to miss. Freeman started down the stairs before remembering that he should wash. He went to the bathroom and wiped his hands and then his clothes with a damp cloth. When he came out, Mom had the phone and was turned facing the kitchen, wiping her forehead with her upper arm.

"It's nice to know you feel like that. . . . I'm listening. I could hang up, you know. . . . I'm willing to listen to reason, certainly. Will you listen also? . . . Fine."

Pop had been standing on the other side of Mom. When he took the phone, Mom switched on the table light. "We decide together. Thirty-five years we've been deciding together. . . . No, I can't. He knows nothing about it as far as we know, except that there was an ac—" Pop saw Freeman easing down the stairs and hung up.

Mom took up a pillowcase from the sewing basket and began stitching on it as if she had to meet a deadline. Pop began switching channels on TV as if he thought it suddenly possible to tune in all of them. On 3, he fiddled with the color, deep garish red, sickly green, dots, lines. Then he started again.

"Where was the call from?" It was as though Freeman had spoken into an empty room. Why didn't they answer? Why had Pop hung up in the middle of a word? And why was it the instant he saw Freeman? The lack of response angered him. "I think I'll go up to Aunt Mag's for a while. Maybe she'll speak to me. Maybe she'll tell me about things. Lots of things." What he had said was being ignored, and he had to have some reaction to prove he was alive and speaking. "You can't bury everything. I'm tired of this old place, and I'm going to leave!"

He moved toward the door, and Pop went to stand against it. He started toward the kitchen, and Mom blocked his way. He knew he wasn't behaving the way they expected him to act, but he had to say something. "I won't be pinned up here any longer. I'll find out about the call. Was it about my dad?"

"Go to your room now, son," Pop said quietly, still ignoring the question. "Go read awhile, then go to bed. Mom and I need to talk." Pop took him by the arm and led him to his room, patting him and saying over and over, "It'll be all right. You'll see. Wait and see."

And Freeman allowed himself to be led, after such a fine show of rage. He grumbled to himself, "You better hush up or put up, my boy." He threw himself on the bed and was ashamed of his bluff, for that surely was what it was. Then he remembered the box in the bathroom closet.

He got the box and dumped its contents on the bed—old Christmas cards and letters, tied in bundles, and a large candy box, red, heart-shaped and with a big red-ribbon rose above the words written on the box: "All my love, Freddy." The box was carefully taped together. When the tape was removed, there were photographs: a plump baby, a plump child of a year, of two years, a slender boy with wagons, tricycles, bicycles. A thin boy on a motorcycle, a girl behind him, a girl with high cheekbones and a broad forehead. Freeman knew this was his mother, for here was his own likeness. He turned the picture over. "Willna Mae" and "Fred" were crayoned inside a red heart. There was a small snapshot of Mae and Fred hugging and moving toward each other in a kiss, against a backdrop of painted palm trees. The picture had been torn through the center, and it was impossible to tell if their lips really met. The tape on it was yellowed and one side of her chin was shattered. But there was Freeman's nose. And Bill Jack Coleman's nose! She must be Bill Jack's daughter, and he must be Bill Jack's grandchild. Freeman sat nodding and shaking his head, having an unspoken conversation with himself. Is this really so? That must be why

Clarence and Bill Jack act as they do toward me. Why Mom doesn't want me talking to them.

He started downstairs with the box, but the lights were out. He had been longer at this than he had thought, and more deeply absorbed in it. He propped the motorcycle picture of his father and mother on the dresser and stared at it from a distance.

How dumb could a fellow be? Had he really been that unsuspecting, or was it that Mom and Pop had kept him so carefully shielded? Impossible, he whispered. But nothing's impossible. Improbable, maybe . . . but true.

"Good night, Daddy and Mother. Good night," he said to the picture. If they were dead, they couldn't be calling. If—why had he used that word? Then who had called? And why had Mom and Pop acted so excited and been so disturbed about the call and about his questions concerning the call? And Pop had hung up saying, "He knows nothing about it as far as we know, except that there was an ac—" The word "accident" fitted. It fitted perfectly.

8

Pop shook him awake the next morning and left, appearing not to have seen the picture on the dresser. The lunch bag was in its usual spot on the corner of the sink. The food on the table had been waiting. There was no steam rising from his oatmeal or his chocolate.

"We all kind of overslept this morning, and you'll have to rush to get to school on time," Mom said.

Perfect attendance was important to her. He hadn't ever missed a day of school, but there had to be a first time for nearly everything. He was opening his mouth to say he was not going to school when Pop said, "We'll talk later. About a lot of things."

Freeman hadn't tasted his food, but his bowl and cup were empty and Mom was saying, "Be careful." She always said it, no matter what he was doing, every time he left the house, as if some danger lurked beyond her immediate vision.

"And you come straight home," Pop said. He

always said that. But he hadn't always looked so old and tired, had he?

Suddenly Freeman decided to follow the creek, as he had the evening he rode Old Nell to Bill Jack's house. He could avoid meeting anyone, avoid having to speak to anyone. If he had to speak, he might cry or tell his problem. And he wasn't exactly certain he knew what it was himself. He simply wanted to be alone.

After going out the front door, he went around the house, down the knoll and across the bottom to the creek. He stood staring into the rusty-looking water, as if it were a crystal ball, until he heard voices. Two men were walking toward the coal dock.

"They say old Highpockets Varney got it for nothing from the Indians. Hundreds of acres for two shotguns and two horses. They sold the mineral, like everybody else did. Used to be sawmills all over and they cut off a fortune in virgin timber. And it's all covered now with good second-growth locust and poplar that'll sell sky high when they want to turn it loose. Some are getting riled up and squawking that they've been robbed. We better get these choice seams stripped in the next year or two. Outsiders coming in, people talking themselves into a tizzy about land damage and pollution, and they may keep on till they get laws which scalp us right out of business. First thing you know, they'll have us saying 'pretty please' for permission to claim what's ours. Bought as fair and square as they bought it, and we're giving them jobs. Stop mining and they'll kill the goose laying the golden eggs. If they'll leave us be, we'll make a lot of level land."

"When're we starting on the new seam?"

"Soon as we get that new auger in and get that lower seam done up the hollow. Maybe auger one more seam, but there's one to be stripped here and one on old lady Blackburn's place. These folks here won't stir up any trouble. Hear they'd walk a mile in the rain to avoid trouble. Real good people who tend to their own business. So if we can do this stretch first, it'll help out with the other seams."

The men turned toward the dock. They were paying Mom and Pop for setting the dock on the land. The hill wasn't being used for anything, and they would pay something for hauling over it, two or three cents a ton. Mom and Pop were always pleased to have money to take to the bank in Centerville. Money had never been a problem, except with Aunt Mag who thought Mom should divide with her. Mom had been paid for nearly a mile of railroad along the edge of the hill. "Living high on the hog," Aunt Mag had said about the railroad, "and I got stuck with the broken end of the stick."

The land along the creek was soft, and Freeman's shoes buried in it two or three times. He washed off the mud when he reached the concrete post which marked the beginning of the school property. He kicked a half-burned milk box into the sodden pile of garbage which had escaped the incinerator.

Home-room period was over when he reached his room.

The day dragged.

"What's the matter?" Birdie asked when they met in the hall. "You look like you lost something. A smile maybe."

Freeman shook his head. His mind was a series of contradictions. Sometimes he wished he hadn't meddled, hadn't searched for the pictures, hadn't eavesdropped. But he also wished he had been more demanding, had said long ago, "Tell me everything, whatever it is. We'll share it. I'm big enough, old enough. Stop treating me like a small child." Maybe he was wrong. Maybe he wasn't old enough to understand whatever it was, but he wanted to try.

Birdie's mother told her children everything. They discussed things, and she tried to answer their questions. Maybe that was the modern way, but Mom and Pop Sloan believed in the old-fashioned way. They believed a child was to be seen more than heard, that grownups had the right and the duty to make decisions, since they knew more from experience than Freeman knew. They wanted to stand between him and anything ugly or frightening for as long as possible. Maybe his problem was not really new at all. Many children were brought up by grandparents. Maybe it was that he was trying to force them into a way of living that they were unprepared for.

Mrs. Philpott said, "Freeman, please pay attention."

He had been staring out the window so hard his eyes hurt and yet he hadn't seen anything really. A train, with its three diesel engines, had dragged several loaded cars slowly around the curve back of the window. The janitor had taken out a load of milk boxes. Nothing new. The social studies class had nothing new either. Students were reading aloud, one paragraph each, up one row and down the next, about raising sheep and cattle in the West.

He remembered a cat they'd had two, maybe three, years ago. Tabby had been dumped out by someone and had found the barn and stayed there several days getting over her fears. Mom accused the cat of scratching up her newly planted flower seeds and shook a broom at her. Tabby looked Mom in the eye, stuck out her tongue, curled it to a pink ribbon and then reached out a white paw and patted the broom. Mom made no claims on the cat, but the cat claimed Mom and followed her about, talking in purrs, meows and rubbings. When they found Tabby in a trap by the creek, Pop said, "Don't tell her, unless you have to. She's mighty attached to the little rascal." Mom also protected Pop. It was their way.

Mrs. Philpott said, "Freeman, would you please stop that?"

Without realizing it, he had been raking his fingernails across the top of his desk.

By afternoon recess, he felt he could not sit there another minute. He got permission to leave and hurried home. The door was locked. He rode his bike around the house. He sat in the swing. He went to the back porch and took a greenish red apple from a bowl on top of the freezer. Crunch, crunch. In the quiet, his chewing sounded like a giant breaking dinosaur bones. A yellowjacket circled him, coming in closer with each orbit. Have an apple, have a yellowjacket. They went together. The cherry tree near the old well box had a web. He looked for a spider. Have a web, have a spider. An awkward mud dauber buzzed into one of the long rows of apartments fastened to the eaves of the house, and some mud dropped on Freeman's hand. He walked across the yard and a flock of grasshoppers rose and flew ahead of him, landed, then took off noisily again. Fish were a school. Cattle were a herd. Birds were a flock. Maybe everything flying in groups made flocks, maybe not. He should look it up. Sometime.

He went to the barn. It was the first time he had been there since losing Old Nell. That was Mom's word, losing. She thought it was less jolting than some other words might be. Old Lead and Stemper, chained to the corner of the barn and resting in the shady hall, got up slowly, stretched and came to him. Their watering pan was overturned. When he filled it, they lapped thirstily. He gave them some dry food which was kept in the barn for supplementing table scraps. They sniffed but did not taste it. Old Lead's black coat shone as if it had been greased. Stemper squatted in the shade and scratched his white belly.

Freeman scolded and wagged a finger. "You better not have fleas."

The wiggle left them. Their tails crept down and curled back between their legs and they looked up at him sorrowfully.

"Can't you take a joke?" Freeman said, laughing. "Old Lead? Stemper? Come on now."

The changed tone of his voice pleased them. He snapped his fingers and they fell over each other trying to get closer to him. He got a brush and gently brushed each dog.

"Freeman?" Pop called.

"Here," Freeman shouted. Sweat ran down his cheeks and seeped into one corner of his mouth as he ran to where Pop was standing in the back yard.

"Saw your books. We hadn't expected you back till school was out. Been up to Mag's."

Aunt Mag's voice carried to the yard. "Now, Viney, you just stop worrying so. You're supposed to shed troubles like a duck does water, shake it off, and you've always let things sink in too deep. Everything'll work out all right, if you'll stop thinking it's a crime when somebody does something the way he sees it instead of the way you see it. Remember the shine you cut when Pa gave me the home place, you a-thinking it was yours because of you being the baby one. Well, you got the potted end of that rainbow, didn't you? Dough sluicing in so fast I hear you've got it in every bank in town."

She continued without a break as Freeman went to stand in the doorway. "You've been a lucky woman, Lavina Sloan, and not enough gray matter upstairs to know it." Mom left for the kitchen but Aunt Mag kept talking without stopping for sentence endings. "Always hard-headed as a turtle. You felt like you had some priority on right judgment."

Pop shook his head and said, "Shhh."

Aunt Mag paid no attention to him. "Chickens always come home to roost sooner or later, I said, didn't I? But even as a youngun she had to hide things. Break a dish and it disappeared. She'd swear up and down, inside and out, that she'd not seen it that morning, or whatever time it was discovered. Things weren't discovered soon as they happened, you know, and that gave her a safe edge on the truth. She had to play her own little game of hide-and-seek. Me, I just owned up to whatever it was and got it over with. They always said, 'That Maggie'd tell the hanging of her own granny,' and if my granny was hung I figured there wasn't a thing to be done about it and no reason to bury her every day." She wiped her forehead. "Figured you'd a had air-conditioning in by now, George. Hear they're putting it in down at the new church."

Pop sat down on the couch. "Don't need it more than a half dozen days a year. Need the exercise fanning can give."

"Can't take it with you, all that money. Oh well." She picked up a newspaper and fanned. "For all, we've had a good family. Nobody ever bootlegged. My Bill's the only one that's double married and your Fred's the only one in the whole gang's ever had trouble with the law." Freeman's mouth fell open here, but she was too busy fanning and talking to notice his reaction. "And I think Willna Mae explained the truth about it, that my Bill gave her some whiskey to break up the flu Fred had taken, and she poured too much of it down him. He evidently went out of his head."

"What did he do?" Freeman asked. Aunt Mag

turned two or three pages of the paper down to make a heavier and less floppy fan. "What'd he do?" he repeated.

"School's out, and I want you to listen to them noisy younguns. When Viney taught, you could a heard a pen drop in the room and almost on the road. Teachers leave the road behavior to the bus drivers and bus drivers leave it to the parents and parents blame it on the school, so they get wilder all the time. I guess I ought to go in and see where Viney's disappeared to."

"I never disappeared," Mom called from the kitchen. "Came in to turn on the fan and decided to do some other things. Go ahead and tell him."

"Well, they went to Chicago where my Bill and Velma lived. Fred lost his job, then he got sick with the flu two weeks after you were born. He drank too much of that whiskey trying to break up the flu. He swore he never remembered a thing about it all. But he tried to rob a grocery store. Got caught because he was shaking so much the man didn't pay any attention to him. He'd picked up Bill's gun and thought it wasn't loaded and it was." Aunt Mag's eyes were taking in the room, examining every chair and lamp, curtain and flowerpot. "I want a slip off that begonia there, Viney."

Pop went to the kitchen and came back with a slice of pineapple upside-down cake. "Sample this.

Viney made it this morning from scratch. Scratched around in a box of cake mix."

Aunt Mag laughed. "Listen to that. You always were a joker, George Sloan."

Freeman wanted to scream. If Pop were a joker, Freeman hadn't noticed it before, and this wasn't the time for jokes. This was serious. This was tragic, and he hated them both for the moment. How could they be so callous? He wanted to shout at them, "Shut up!" That moment passed while Aunt Mag slit the cake in the middle, quartered it and speared the first slice with a fork. They had known this story for years, he realized then; the misery and disappointment had had time to become dulled with them. And maybe they were trying to make it a little easier for him.

He waited patiently for Aunt Mag to finish the cake and to make a detour into her own life—how poor Will, her husband, had loved pineapple and them unable to buy it and how the Sandy Mine cave-in took his life along with that of a brother and several neighbors. She kept chasing cake crumbs and finding new layers to her own problems until Freeman felt he could not bear to sit still any longer. He contracted and released his toes to keep his feet from going to sleep. He stretched and stood. He changed chairs. At last he said, "Go on, Aunt Mag. I want to know all about it."

"I know you do, you poor little thing. All these years, I've tried to tell them, but they wouldn't listen. You had a right to know the truth. Not many people ever knew anything about it, the trial being in Chicago and all. Billy's been suspicious of a lot, but he never has really known. Pestered me nearly to death, the little bugger, asking questions. A few times I've got mad enough at Viney to choke her half to death, and her my own sister. She always felt a little blameful toward me because Bill and Freddy were so close and then Bill married Velma and all. And the gun was Bill's, you see, besides the whiskey. Fred was wild about Willie Mae and paid no mind to nobody. Broke George and Viney's heart, but they tried to do the best they could. I know that. They went up there and stood by him during the trial. And they've worried all these years, though they've tried not to show it. But now that he's getting out and they're coming back, George and Viney can't hide it any longer."

"We've tried," Pop said. "We really have."

Aunt Mag nodded her head. "But I have to admit, I never felt you gave them any credit, after they got married, for trying to make a go of it. And they were trying. In their own way."

9

It took intense concentration to stay with Aunt Mag through her many detours. At times Freeman's thoughts took off on bits of the story and came back to find that he had lost out on some of it. But he did not interrupt, and after a while she decided to make a long story shorter. "You were a tiny baby, and she'd just come home from the hospital with you, and Fred was upset at not being able to provide for you and her in the way he'd been used to living at home. He couldn't have earned enough even to pay the rent on a house like this. And he was sick after losing his job. And that's it in a nut shell."

Aunt Mag reached across the bookcase beside her. "What did I do with my glasses?" She patted her lap, came up with the glasses and said, "If they'd been a snake, I'd a been bit for sure and certain. Viney, I'd better be going."

"Why don't you and Billy come back for supper? Got enough."

"That sounds more like you, Viney, than you've

sounded in quite a spell, but I'd better stay home, I guess. I sure am glad Fred's getting out of prison. That poor boy's suffered enough, and more than enough. And them hoping to come home, and all, I do hope everything works out all right. Well, I'm gone now."

Freeman sat there in a kind of daze. It was as if a stone had been thrown through a window and pieces of glass were still falling around him. The father and mother he'd thought dead were alive! It had all been a little too much to understand. As Aunt Mag put it, "A pretty big dose to swallow." Maybe the first jolt had been like the needle that numbed one for surgery. He certainly felt numb now.

He was aware of Mom and Pop going to sit on the back porch. They had been keeping the knowledge from him because it hurt them and because they had known it would hurt him. His father had married a bootlegger's fourteen-year-old daughter, had gone off to a strange city, had committed a crime. His father was an armed robber! And somewhere in her long retelling of the story, Aunt Mag had said, "Mae and Fred said to consider them dead, and George and Viney took them at their word."

It was all too much to absorb at one time. Freeman clenched and unclenched his fists. He pushed against the floor, as if he could make a hole in it and sink through the hole. If he climbed onto a chair, perhaps he could knock a hole in the ceiling and let pain cancel out the strangeness he felt inside.

At supper, Mom and Pop seemed more relaxed than he had ever seen them. Still, they passed baked squash and fall beans back and forth endlessly, it seemed to Freeman.

This, he knew, was a way of postponing what must be said. Aunt Mag had been a go-between in revealing the events which had separated all of them. Aunt Mag had made a crack in the wall. He would have to push the shattered pieces back until there was an opening large enough to reach through.

"Please talk to me," he said.

Then Mom said, "Freeman, we've tried to provide a good home, hoped to give the happiness and security we thought you needed. Maybe these things can't be given. Anyway, we've tried to provide the atmosphere where they could develop. Perhaps we were wrong to hide all this from you. Try and remember we did what we thought right, what seemed right to us. For all these years we've cared, maybe too much, and maybe you can't ever care too much. I don't know. Caring's not a thing you can measure very well, not ever something to be estimated in what's enough or not enough."

Freeman said, "I know," although he really didn't know. When they had finished eating, he said, "And Bill Jack Coleman's my grandfather?"

Pop nodded. "Big Bill married Velma Coleman.

Fred and Bill were pals. Bill and Velma went to Chicago."

Mom took up the story. "But not until they'd stayed at Mag's awhile and got Fred and Willna Mae started seeing each other. Mag harbored them up there and never let us know about it until they were ready to marry. Bill Jack went with them to Virginia and signed that Mae was sixteen so they could marry. Fred was eighteen, had just started college in Centerville. Besides our wanting him to go to school and wait awhile on marriage, we didn't want him to choose her. She was poor as Job's turkey and hadn't even finished high school. And her daddy had just been released from prison for making and selling whiskey. They were too young, though, was the main thing. Children."

"One of the pictures I found showed them on a motorcycle," Freeman said.

Pop crossed his knife and fork, rearranged the salt and pepper shakers. "Taken on Boldmans Branch where Bill Jack lived. Fred was threatening that he'd not start college, and we bought the motorcycle, trying to please him. But you can't buy obedience. They stayed with us a few days after they were married, them feeling all angry because we'd been against the marriage, nagging, hinting that we should set them up in a fine house and buy them a new car and give them money to live on while they finished school. And we'd told Fred before he mar-

ried that we wouldn't do that. Then they stayed a
few days at Bill Jack's and took off for Chicago.
We've had to consider that if we'd given in, things
might've been different. We didn't, because it didn't
seem right."

"And Fred—my daddy's been in prison for armed
robbery?"

Mom stacked the dishes at the table. "On a charge
of armed robbery. I believe that he didn't know the
gun was loaded and that he didn't know, at the
minute, what he was doing. Then in the courthouse, she was blaming us and said, 'I never want to
see you again. Consider me dead.' And he said,
'Make it double. I'm dead too.' It hurt. It still hurts.
But they made the choice."

Pop turned to Mom. "Let the dishes go, and rest
awhile."

"I'll do the dishes." Freeman had to swallow
twice before he could ask, "Didn't they want me?"

"They knew you'd be better off with us. We
asked them to leave you with us and not to bother
you, a little tiny thing, not much bigger than a craw-
dad. Willna Mae was just a child, remember, with
no money and no way of taking care of you. Bill and
Velma had already broken up and Velma was influ-
encing Mae. But they've kept up with you by writ-
ing to Bill Jack and Mag."

Freeman went to the living room after he had
finished washing the dishes. "One more question,"

he said, "and then I'll let you rest. It was her—my mother—who called?"

Pop nodded and leaned back heavily on the couch. "Fred's out, and they're coming back. Said Bill Jack invited them to live at his house but that they probably couldn't get along with Cassie and would wind up living under a rock cliff. She was exaggerating. Mae speaks like that. Said they were going to start over. Can't start over. But maybe we can all start at some even point." Pop lay down on the couch. "She's strong-willed. There's nothing we could do to stop their coming back, if we wanted to, and we don't want to. We were going to tell you soon anyway."

"I can't figure out why you tried to keep it a secret in the first place." This wasn't what he'd meant to say. He was beginning to understand. Would he have understood if they'd told him that his father was in prison and that his mother was staying far away so as to be near his father? What difference would it have made? He couldn't decide now. But he needed to console Mom and Pop, to let them know he was not condemning them, not even judging them. "It's been a nice twelve years," he said. "When will they be here?"

Mom picked up her knitting and laid it down again. She picked a thread from the rug, then wiped her face on her apron.

Pop answered, "Didn't say. Maybe a day or so. I

guess you know by now why we've felt so cold toward Bill Jack. His knowing we were against the marriage and forging that paper. If we'd thought it would've done any good, we'd a tried to have the marriage annulled. Still, he's got a right to his feelings."

"Are you defending him?" Mom scolded. "Saying because he thinks something's right makes it right?"

"Now you know I never said that."

"Anybody could maybe put it together and say you did." Mom rocked back and forth. "But even the devil deserves his due. So far as I know, he's gone straight since he got out of the bootlegging."

Pop shook his head at Mom. "Remember, the least said the soonest mended. I wish I knew if they'd started, what they plan to do. Of course, what they plan's their own business, and I doubt they'll be inviting our counsel. Still, we need to allow for change and be open-minded."

"I tried to be so open-minded once my mind felt like a sieve. Fred's a man now. She's a woman. And we may be bigger 'old fogies' than ever."

Freeman watched as Mom picked up the sweater again. "We cried our eyes out, but that was before you can remember. Bedtime now, I guess. Lyingdown time anyway, boys."

Freeman went to bed knowing that all their lives would be changed in many ways by whatever Fred and Willna Mae Sloan decided. He had wanted change, had sometimes resented the sameness of his life, and now that change was evident, he wished it would be only a small one. He almost wished that things could return to what they had been, that he could retreat behind Mom and Pop and not have to face these strangers who would be appearing in his life. He didn't really need a father and mother, not with Mom and Pop. He didn't want to see Mom and Pop hurt more than they already had been. The faces in the photographs were young, but that was years ago. What would they be like now? They might be hardened criminals. What if they planned to bootleg whiskey? They might try to kidnap him, or rob Mom and Pop. It was all too big a subject to follow tonight. And maybe they would decide not to come back to Toms Creek after all.

His thoughts ran like a river, and his body rolled and tossed with them.

After a while, Pop called, "What's wrong, son? Something hurting you?"

He hadn't known anything was hurting, but it was. He barely had time to reach the bathroom before his supper came up.

Mom fixed him a fizzy glass of sugar water, vinegar and baking soda and sat beside him while he drank it. "Maybe something you ate. My stomach's always been upset when my emotions are upset. Try

121

not to think about it any more tonight and don't worry." Mom gave a little laugh. "I'm a good one to tell anyone not to worry, when I'm a regular worry-wart. Maybe it'd be more sensible to say don't worry any more than you have to."

The next morning Freeman wasn't sure whether he had slept at all. The room had been filled with moonlight and ghosty shadows. Had Mom come in and talked with him, or had it been a dream? He thought she'd said, "We tried to give him every-thing, but it wasn't really a gift, I can see now. Some of it was a bribe maybe, because we were selfish and proud and expected loyalty and obedience in return. We failed. And maybe we've failed you too, son, but we can honestly say we've tried to do right. Just know we love you. And we love Fred. Let's hope with all our might things'll work out right, even if it's not the way we think is right." In a moment of silence, he had sensed all the love and disappoint-ment and loneliness of twelve years for her and Pop. "Please understand that we never meant anything but good for Fred and you. We wanted you to have as good a childhood as we could offer. Whatever happens now, we've had these years together."

Was she leaving when she stooped and kissed him and said, "Understand?" Or did he dream it and wake himself answering, "I'm trying Mom, I really am."

They needed rest from talking and maybe from thinking. At breakfast the conversation centered on the weather and the potatoes they planned to dig that day.

As they finished, Pop said, "If anything comes up, let's keep in touch. I think I ought to go down to Uncle Ike's before he sells out and get us some molasses, four or five gallons."

Then Birdie was calling, "Hey, Freeman, you ready?"

Freeman shouted, "Be right with you. Mom, is my lunch packed?"

"No, I've been too addle-brained to get organized this morning. Can you eat in the cafeteria?"

"I guess so. Good-by." Freeman couldn't remember ever having hugged either of them in the morning. Now he leaned over the table and gathered both of them in one giant outspread of arms, squeezed them together and was gone. "Thought you rode the bus," he said to Birdie.

"Did to here. I pretended I had to stop at the store. I wanted to congratulate you."

"On what?"

"Oh, you know." When Freeman shrugged, Birdie said, "You don't mean they're still keeping you in the dark?"

"Don't you say anything about Mom and Pop," Freeman growled. Suddenly the misty rain which had been falling increased to giant-sized drops, and Freeman used it as an excuse for running. Running would prevent their talking. He wanted to postpone talking until he knew what to say: it was all still too personal to share, even with a best friend. "Come on, hurry, Let's get out of the rain."

"You're neither sugar nor salt."

Freeman made a little clucking-shame sound at Birdie. He was sorry that Birdie wanted to talk this morning. He did not feel up to discussing his family. This must be the way Mom and Pop had felt when he had wanted them to talk about what they had called "the accident."

Freeman propped his foot on a stone and stood looking down the hill at the weed-grown land between the Sloan house and the school grounds. When Birdie reached him, he said, "Thought you planned on going to school today."

"Well, we'll not melt. I just happen to like walking in the rain, and it can't hurt my looks."

Birdie gave him a searching look. "Freeman, anything wrong that I can help with?"

Freeman shook his head. "How'd you know?"

"Somebody happened to hear Maggie Blackburn on the phone, talking to Bill Jack. You know how she can talk. Everybody on the creek must know by now. My mom says Mag missed her calling—should a been a preacher or salesman."

124

"She ought to know you can't discuss things on the phone."

"She forgets. Mom says some people are born talkers, some thinkers and some doers and everybody ought to be all three sometimes. Guess which one I am?"

"Which one what?"

Birdie grinned mischievously. "Let me tell you, old pal, I think your mom must pack your wits each morning in that lunch bag, and you ought not go far without them." Birdie gave Freeman a whack across the seat of the pants. He blew a giant bubble, drew it back and let it dangle for a second. "What're you going to do?"

Freeman shook his head. "Did you know? Before now?"

"No, sure didn't." They reached the basketball goal where some first-grade boys were kicking the ball. "Want to shoot? You boys know you're not to kick the basketball," he scolded.

"Tattletale, tattletale, cut his throat and never fail," one of the boys chanted. "I bet Freeman Sloan knows what kind of bird can't fly." He stuck out his tongue.

Birdie said, "Cut it out, you little snipe-catcher. If it turns cold and you freeze like that your own mommy won't claim you." He winked at Freeman and whispered, "Watch them fall for this trick. Say, boys, I see why you've not been hitting the basket. It needs a left-handed monkey wrench took to it. If you guys'll go tell the janitor you need one, I'll fix it." They took off in a hurry. "Last week Billy got rid of them by sending them after a bucket of steam and the janitor sent them right back for a bottomless bucket to put the steam in."

Billy and G.C. came charging at them. "What're you up to?"

"Let's go. Act like we never heard," Freeman said.

"Enough's enough and too much is nasty." Birdie stepped forward, aimed and made a basket. "Not on your life." He caught the rebound and turned to Billy. "Did I hear something or was that a wind passing by?" Birdie danced on his toes, swung the ball from one hand to the other, made a pass as if to toss it to Billy, dribbled it forward and then back between his own legs. Birdie's voice was high and squeaky. "Must be a mouse nibbling at my sugar-candy house."

Billy puffed himself with air like a bullfrog and demanded, "You take that ball from the younguns?"

"And what if I did? They have their rubber balls and are supposed to play on the other side of the building." Birdie shot another basket, caught the ball and handed it to Freeman. "Here, hotshot. Give these kids a demonstration."

Freeman dribbled to the left and made a shot.

The ball spun around the edge before drooping into the basket.

Billy rolled his eyes and opened his mouth in mock surprise. "Well, what do you know? Mom's baby can do all that."

Freeman threw the ball. "Let's see what Aunt Mag's little blessing can do. How many points did you make last year, big'n?"

"You're afraid to come out for the team, both of you," Billy said.

Birdie picked up the books they had stacked beside the goal post. "Kid stuff. We got bigger fish to fry. You'd be shook up if you knew what-all we find to do while you're fumbling that ball." Birdie's mother worked evenings at a restaurant in Centerville and he had to babysit, but he never gave that as an excuse: it would be more bait for teasing.

"Hear somebody's got company coming." When Freeman ignored him, G.C. said, "I say, I hear you got kinfolks heading up the big road." He deliberately fumbled the ball and knocked a notebook from Birdie's hand and stepped on it. "Cat's got somebody's tongue."

"Lay off," Birdie said.

"What's it to you?" Billy asked. "See no evil, hear no evil, Goody Sloan. So what's he going to do about it?" Billy was so close he sprayed Freeman's face with spit as he spoke. When he saw it, he said,

"Double dare you to try and make me take anything back!" He started running.

The spit was warm when it struck Freeman. Then it was like bits of ice on his eyelashes. He started after Billy. Billy dodged behind G.C., went down the center of the court and behind the building. Freeman saw Birdie following and called, "Go back, I can handle this." He wasn't certain if this was a brag or a threat. Billy was bigger and possibly stronger due to playing basketball. The only thing to his own advantage, Freeman knew, was his disgust with Billy. It was more of a teasing game with Billy than a quarrel. Now that Freeman knew the truth about his family, he was not so much angry as shocked that Billy could be small enough to take pleasure in taunting him. He was tired of it.

He gained slowly. When Billy neared the creek bank, Freeman paused to choose the shortest direction and catch his breath. Billy leaped over a log and ran along the sandy edge of the water. Freeman measured the distance and sprinted in a straight line.

He caught Billy by the shirt, and Billy turned with an upraised fist. Freeman dodged it, still holding on. He was too tired to lift the other hand in a fist.

"Take it back!" he panted.

Billy's breathing was even harder. "Why don't you hit me?"

"Don't want to smash you and ruin a good day's schooling."

"I bet the bell's rung. I bet we get the dickens for being tardy." Billy dropped to the ground quickly.

Freeman held on, shaking Billy. "Take it back or hit me."

"Heck, I couldn't hit a flea if it lit on my hand."

"Then you take it back?"

He fell on Billy, grabbing Billy's hands and pressing them into the sand. "Say it, say it before I grind you into bug dust."

Billy tried to move and could not. He heaved again, gathered some spit and held it on his lips. Freeman shook him. "Dare? You don't dare! I'll chop you into bits and feed you to the buzzards!"

"Backtrack. I take it back." Billy grinned up at him.

Warily keeping his balance, Freeman turned and dropped to the ground. He was not certain that Billy would not take advantage of any sign of relaxation. For years there had been a lot of questions he wanted to ask Billy. Sometimes he had imagined himself getting Billy's back to the wall and cutting him down with words, then with fists. Now it didn't matter. Billy rubbed his hands in the dry sand between them. Freeman sat ready to duck in case the sand suddenly flipped toward him.

Billy dug his feet into the ground. "You know something, we should have a track team. Basketball doesn't take in enough fellows. High jump and track. Why don't we ask about it? How'd you ever get up all that wind for running? I thought you were a softie!"

Freeman almost said, "From going for Old Nell in the pasture," but he wasn't ready to discuss Old Nell. "I'd like to get one thing straight."

Billy spread his arms in an exaggerated gesture. "Anything, anything a-tall."

"Why're you always picking on me?"

"You think you're too good to associate with me."

"I do not."

"Then why don't we associate any more? I mean like—why don't you visit me and I visit you?"

"Because of—oh, you ought to know now. Now if you didn't before."

"Swear I didn't really know. Added up things I overheard and tongue-slips Grandma made and knew there was a snake in the grass somewhere. Guess I added it up worse than it was. You know, like two and two makes twenty-two. But when I tried to make Grandma tell me, she said that she'd break my neck if she ever heard of me pestering you."

"Is that the truth?"

Billy reared up angrily. "You accusing me of lying?"

130

"No, but it seems—I don't know—seems nearly impossible to believe that it was a secret so long, about my mother and my daddy."

"Not impossible. No. I tried to question Bill Jack, and he wouldn't tell me anything. Clarence didn't even know, but he's too dumb to come in out'n the rain. Bill Jack wanted to protect you, same as Aunt Viney. And Grandma gripes and nags at Aunt Viney, but she promised not to let it out. The rest of the people didn't know anything, only if a stray word got out and they wondered some, you know."

"Then why have you been so—" Freeman searched for the right word. He wasn't pleased with it, but the one that best fitted the situation was "rotten." "Why've you been so rotten to me?"

"I think you've been the rotten one, Freeman Sloan."

Freeman got to his feet. He clenched his fists. "Put up them fists or shut up, Billy Blackburn, and I don't mean maybe."

"Oh, come off it. I don't want to hurt you." Billy laughed. "You've got that Coleman temper, boy. Underneath all that easy-going attitude, you're hot as a firecracker. I just like to see you get hot under the collar." He scratched his ankle. "May get poison ivy. Something bit me or something."

"What's G.C. got against me?"

"Nothing. I just say, 'There go the birdies,' and

131

he's ready to go along with me. Just something to do, you know. We're going to get our hides tanned if we don't get back. Say, look at that."

A chipmunk was sitting on a log, looking at them, its black eyes shining like two beads, the arch of its back questioning their right to be there.

Billy reached for it. It scrambled up his arm, ripping his shirt across the shoulder and leaving two long scratches. He shouted, "Wowee. Oh, wow, it's beginning to sting. You know something, nobody'll ever believe it."

"What people think and the truth's not always the same. I won't take any blame or any credit for it. I'll tell them."

"Nah, they won't believe it, no matter who tells it."

They walked slowly and companionably across the school ground, while Billy spoke of his worry about his own mother, now living in California.

When they reached the room, Mrs. Philpott asked, "What hurt your arm?"

Billy looked down. The streaks were very red now, and a thin rim of white skin stood up along the edges of each one. "Would you believe a chipmunk?" he asked.

"Would you believe a chipmunk?" two or three of the boys repeated, G.C. among them. Then the class roared with laughter.

10

When Freeman answered the telephone that after-noon, Aunt Mag said, "Honey, you tell Viney we're coming down for a while."

In a few minutes she was there. Billy came loping ahead of her and sat down beside Freeman and in front of the TV as if he did this regularly.

Aunt Mag was a little breathless, but she began calling before Mom could get away from the egg whites she was beating. "Viney, Willna's been try-ing to get hold of you-all, but your line's busy. They're in Centerville. I think what she really wanted to ask was for George to come over and pick them up. Bill Jack got over there and burned the transmission out of his old truck and he's going to try to work on it."

"She had the habit of telling us what to do."

"Now, Viney, let bygones be bygones, can't you?"

"I'm willing to try my level best. Why didn't Fred call?"

"Oh well, I didn't ask her that and she didn't volunteer to tell it." Aunt Mag sighed. "She gave me the bus station number so you could call, if you'd a mind to."

Mom picked up the telephone. "Could I use it for a minute, please? Then you can have it back." She dialed. "Willna? . . . We're fine. . . . If Fred's handy, put him on. . . . Fred? You want your daddy to come after you? . . . He's down in the lower garden fixing a post one of the coal trucks knocked loose, but you don't have to ask him. . . . Well, all right. Freeman, go and call Pop to come to the phone."

As they went through the kitchen, Billy paused to lick the spoon Mom had been using. "You think he'll tell us about the robbery? Boy, that must've been exciting," he said.

The post cemented in, Pop was already on his way to the house. "Telephone," Billy called. "Freeman, you think he'll tell us about things?"

"Now how would I know?" Freeman said a little irritably. "You know him as well as I do." He rushed back to the house, not wanting to miss a word of the conversation.

"It'll take about an hour over and back. Mag and I'll cook supper. . . . Now, Fred, it won't be all that much trouble, if you can wait that long to eat. Here's your daddy."

Pop listened, then said, "Be glad to. . . . No, no, it won't be any trouble. . . . Well, we're all well as common. I'll start right now. . . . He's right here. Freeman?" Pop held the telephone out to him.

A strange voice said, "Son, are you all right?"

Freeman's voice shook as he said, "I'm fine." There was a long silence. He didn't know what to say. If no one had been listening, he might have said: Don't talk about it, if you don't want to. But more likely he would have said: Don't hurt Mom and Pop and don't change things, not any more than you have to.

The voice said, "Are you there?"

"Yes."

"Your mother wants to speak to you."

Another strange voice, a quicker one, said, "Freeman, what're you doing?"

"Nothing. Just standing here holding the phone." It was a silly answer, when she obviously knew that, and perhaps meant him to tell her what he'd been doing when he was asked to speak, or maybe about some big project of some kind. But he couldn't think of anything to tell her, not with Mom and Billy and Aunt Mag hovering over him.

"We'll be seeing you in a little while, and I can't wait. Son, you sound like a little boy."

"Yes?"

"Well, see you soon."

He hung up. Pop had already started. The truck was pulling out of the drive. Mom and Aunt Mag went to the kitchen, and Freeman sat down, weak in the knees.

"What did they say?" Billy asked.

"Nothing."

"Oh, they had to say something."

"Just the usual." Freeman shrugged a little, hoping to give the impression that everything was fine, that it was a simple experience to speak with a mother and a father you'd never seen and hadn't known existed until a couple of days ago.

Above the noise of the TV, Freeman could hear Mom and Aunt Mag talking about Fred's liking potato salad. It all seemed unreal to him.

When the cartoon ended, Billy and Freeman went upstairs. Billy tried out the bed and the chair, saying over and over, with amazement in his voice, "Boy, isn't that something?"

Freeman demonstrated the FM on his radio since Billy was thinking of buying a radio and wasn't sure of the kind he wanted. They went through Freeman's comic books and Billy chose a half dozen for borrowing. They played a game of checkers half way through and decided they were both too excited for the game to be interesting.

"Boy, I remember the time Daddy brought his new wife home, and I'd already decided I'd hate her, maybe not really hate her, but I didn't plan on trying to like her. We liked her though, in spite of ourselves, Grandma and me. You know something, I talked to Mr. Daniels and he said he'd really like to start a track team, maybe a high jump."

"Why'd you make up your mind not to like me? From my side of the fence, you've given me a pretty rough time. I never could figure it out."

"Aw, it's not been all that bad. I guess because Aunt Viney thought you too good to associate with me."

"Watch your tongue, Billy Blackburn. She did not. She was just afraid you knew something about my parents that I didn't know and might tell it. And disturb me."

"Now, your mother and mine're sisters. But I swear I didn't know it. Aunt Viney just wouldn't let you out from behind the door."

Billy paused and Freeman wanted to protest. But he was determined to make a special effort to get along with Billy—to bend over backward, Pop would have said.

"My grandma got miffed at yours about the land and all, and they've pouted, you know. But she'd promised Aunt Viney that she'd not say anything about your daddy and mother, so every few days she'd say, 'Now you be dead certain and sure you don't go saying anything to Freeman.' And I couldn't figure out what it was. See, it all happening up in Chicago, there wasn't an awful lot of people around here knew about it."

Billy stood by the window, leaning out. Somebody went walking up the road and he called, "Yahoo," and ducked back into the room. "I've never fooled around much up at Bill Jack's. Grandma never said I couldn't or anything, but I can't stand that lousy Clarence. I asked him once why he acted so tough and he said it was because I acted like I thought I was something on a Christmas tree. 'Stuck up,' he said. 'You and that Freeman Sloan's both so stuck up I could use you for wallpaper and not have to have any glue.' And Bill Jack. I wouldn't more'n get there till he'd start asking about you, and that made me kind of suspicious about something. So I'd bait you. Pure curiosity on my part and a little streak of meanness, and the way you'd rather be with Birdie Powell. My mother and yours— sisters. What kin does that all make us?"

"I don't know."

"Stop saying 'I don't know.' Aunt Viney's—"

"Don't you say anything about my grandmother, Billy Blackburn," Freeman said fiercely.

"And don't you say anything about mine!"

They were arguing again, but more peacefully this time, and with more understanding.

"Grandma said yesterday, 'Billy, why don't you

try to like Freeman?' and I said, 'I already do. He's all right.' And you are. I guess you just naturally don't talk as much as I do. More easy-going like, or something."

"Thanks."

"Why don't we go down to the barn and put up a hoop for a basket and that way you can get in some ball practice?"

Freeman looked out the window. "Too dark now. Pop never did put lights down there."

"Tomorrow then?"

Tomorrow was far away. Too much depended on the next few hours. Freeman shivered a little with anxiety. "Maybe. Let's wait and see how things turn out."

"What do you reckon made him do it, rob the store?"

"How would I know?" It was a sore subject. Freeman couldn't bear thinking about it.

"Reckon he'll tell us about it, what it's like and all? Wonder why he decided to come back here? I'm excited, aren't you?"

"Yeah, sure I'm excited. I'm not going to ask."

"Grandma said he'd been sick and needed some rest. Think he volunteered for some medicine in prison. You know, for testing something. Are you going to leave your grandma?" Billy was so wrapped up in what he was saying that he didn't seem to notice when Freeman didn't answer. "Aunt Willie called Grandma and said they were going to Bill Jack's. Might do you good to see how the other side lives." Billy stretched out on the bed.

An automobile came up the road. Freeman held his breath. It passed the house, its brake lights winking on and off as it slowed for bumps in the road.

After what seemed like hours had passed, Freeman heard Pop slam the truck door. There was a strange voice in the house. "Anybody home?"

"Fred," Mom said.

"Fred," Aunt Mag echoed.

Freeman and Billy walked to the top of the stairs, then began easing down them. Freeman could see that the dining room table had a white cloth and dishes on it. In the kitchen Mom was being rocked back and forth in the arms of a tall thin man. By moving one step to the left, Freeman could see the kitchen door where a woman was standing not quite inside. She was short, dark-skinned, and with long dark hair falling across the front of a white blouse.

Mom turned and said, "Mae, you come on in."

Freeman wouldn't have known this was his father and his mother, not from the photographs. These were strangers. These were people he wouldn't have noticed on the street. People who might change his entire life. For a minute he wished he could close his eyes and make them go away. Then he was ashamed of himself. He had waited and wondered so long. Now they were here, but he did not feel the surge of joy he had thought he might feel. The shyness he had believed might go away at first sight of them was still there, only bigger and deeper.

Aunt Mag went running toward them with a bag of frozen rolls in her hand. She kissed them both and momentarily hid them from his sight. Freeman looked at Mom. She had stepped to the corner of the stove and was wiping her face on a towel that hung from the rack he had given her one Christmas.

"Are we welcome here?" the woman asked.

"Willna Mae," Mom said shakily, "don't talk like that."

Freeman's mother stood there, a broader and heavier woman than Mom Sloan, twisting her hands together nervously. She wet her lips slowly and completely before saying, "Mrs. Sloan, there's not been enough real talk between us. You've hurt us, and we've hurt you. I don't intend to try and say who's right or wrong, but I don't want to force myself on you if I'm not welcome."

Pop said, "We don't have to talk about anything past now. Come on in and sit down and rest. Like I told you both on the way here, there's no rush for going into whys and what-fors. We can talk things over when the right time comes. Now, where's that boy? Freeman?"

Freeman meant to enter with great dignity and show how grown-up he was. Instead, he skidded on a scatter rug, slammed into the wall and very nearly fell on his face.

The woman came toward him with both hands out, saying, "My baby? My baby all grown up?" She bent over him, her hands on his shoulders, and it was too much, too much too fast. He looked away, staring at a peanut-butter stain he'd made on the wall, while she said, "How are you, Freeman?"

"I'm fine," he said. It did not seem enough, that bare answer, and he added, "Everything's fine. Only we lost Old Nell a few days ago." Now why on earth did he say that? "And this is Billy." He pointed to where Billy was standing, staring at the ceiling and at that minute saying, "Oh, mush."

The woman moved to one side and Fred Sloan knelt beside him, took his face between his hands and held it so he could look Freeman in the eyes. "Willie Mae, he looks like you. Son, you're a big boy. I still thought of you as a little boy, a tiny baby." Fred dropped his head to Freeman's shoulder. Freeman stood very still, then he grew tired and wondered if the man had fallen asleep.

Mom had been watching. Maybe she saw that Freeman was tired and bewildered. She said, "Pop, you all could go and sit in the living room while Mag and I set up supper. I know Fred and Mae are tired after that long trip. We'll have it ready in a minute."

"Be ready quicker'n a sheep can shake its tail," Aunt Mag said.

They went to the living room, the woman leading Freeman by the hand. He would have preferred to stay in the kitchen and help Mom. Pop's chair squeaked. The clock on the wall roared. Freeman stood by the couch, his hand still being held, and tried to see what Billy was finding so interesting in the TV program.

Willna Mae said, "Well, we're here at last."

Billy asked, "How's my dad?"

"Fine. Everybody's fine," Fred said.

"That's good," Pop said.

Freeman's hand grew sweaty. Billy pulled a footstool closer to the TV. Fred crossed and uncrossed his legs. Willna Mae traced the design on the couch cover with her free hand. And there didn't seem to be anything to talk about until Mom called them to the table.

"We've had supper, but I always eat with a coming appetite," Aunt Mag said, laughing at the heap of food on her plate.

They spoke politely of food prices, the weather and traffic, with a lot of "pleases" and "thank yous," with long silences between.

Aunt Mag finished eating first. She patted back a yawn. "My years are overtaking me, and it's time I went to roost. Who's going up to make out a night batching with Billy and me?"

"Thanks, Aunt Mag," Fred said, "but we'd better take a rain check on that. I hear they're getting ready to open a mine on you."

"Been augering a couple of days."

Billy poked Freeman. "Dare me to ask him something?"

Freeman shook his head and drew his lips together firmly.

Billy began, "Aunt Willie Mae—" and Freeman poked him.

She didn't appear to notice that Billy had spoken. She said, "Daddy's planning on us coming to his house. I'll help Mrs. Sloan clear away the dishes first."

"I'll take care of the dishes," Mom said, "but I'd rather you didn't go off tonight. Your room's still up there. And, Mae, you can call me whatever you like, but you're as much Mrs. Sloan as I am."

"Well, I'm standing here trading early bedtime to late. I better be going," Aunt Mag said.

Billy got up from the table with a chicken breast in his hand. "See you tomorrow, Freeman?"

"See you tomorrow. You'll come down?" Freeman answered.

He had been shrinking a little. Would they go off, after twelve years of being gone? Surely they didn't think he'd leave Mom and Pop tonight. He hadn't thought they would dream of going anywhere. But how could he imagine what two strange people would do?

There was a tense silence after Aunt Mag and Billy left. Fred went to the kitchen for a drink and Willna Mae followed. They were gone so long Freeman began thinking they had already left.

Then they were back, standing in the middle of the room, and Fred asked, "Do you think I could get a job at one of the coal docks, Dad? Have to be light work for a while."

"You might, but they don't hire many people with the mining they do now." Pop leaned back and stretched his legs. "We're all real glad you decided to come back home."

"Couldn't find work, and Bill Jack wrote that we were welcome at his place. He's adding on a room for us."

"You don't have to go up there, you know. I told them on the way here, Viney, that they were welcome to stay with us long as they want to. Why, I remember a few years ago that a lot of people married and never did move out."

Mom nodded quickly. Fred shook his head slowly several times. "Things've changed. We don't want to impose on anybody."

Willna Mae moved a step toward the door. "Freeman acts like he's scared to death. Come over here, honey."

Freeman did not move. He was not ready to go from a motherless boy to one with a "honey" and a smothering hug this quickly. He needed time to adjust.

Nervous with anticipation, Willna Mae thought he was rejecting her, that he had been coached in his actions toward them. She turned toward Mom and said, "You've turned him against us. You've taught him to act like this. You took him and then turned him against us."

Mom looked at her squarely. "Don't start that kind of foolishness. You didn't have a way of keeping him and were crying, 'What'll I do with the baby?' and I said, 'Give him to us,' and you did, right in that courthouse in Chicago. He's tired now and not used to staying up this late."

Willna Mae took a step toward Mom, and Freeman jumped between them. "You don't quarrel at Mom," he said. "She's good to me."

"Freeman, son," Fred said quietly, "you're talking to your mother."

"And she's quarreling at Mom. Please don't quarrel." Freeman's voice shook with fear that they would come between him and his grandparents. He wanted to love them, these strangers, but it would take time. He could not turn his affections for them on as if those affections were a water faucet or a light switch. "Please don't quarrel," he repeated weakly.

His mother was not looking at him now, did not appear to have heard him. "Fred, we'd better go. Freeman, let's go up to Daddy's and spend the night." She turned back to him, her voice soft, her hands upturned and reaching toward him. "They'll be expecting all of us. It'll be a good experience for you to spend a night away—away from . . . here."

"Wait a minute," Pop said, standing. "I could drive up there and tell them you're all staying here."

"No," Willna Mae said firmly. "We're not waiting. We're going to Daddy's this minute. We want Freeman to go with us, and he wants to go, don't you, son?"

"Fred, I'll take you and Mae," Pop said hurriedly. "And remember, like I said on the way here, Freeman's going to have the right to make up his own mind."

Fred walked closer, lay his hand on Freeman's head. "Get your things to take."

The words were spoken so quietly and so softly that Freeman thought at first the man was speaking to someone else or about something else. When he recognized what they meant, he stiffened, felt the top of his head pressing against the hand. He thought of saying, "What things? Take where?" Instead, he moved away without speaking.

"You want to stay with us, don't you?" Fred asked.

"You can stay here," Freeman answered.

"We can't, after promising Bill Jack. You're not going to treat us that way, are you?"

Freeman moved a step backward and stood between Mom's and Pop's chairs. He was tired, too tired to go anywhere. He shrugged and held onto Mom's chair.

"Freeman?" When he failed to answer, his mother said, "It's hard to tell what they've told him, to turn him against us. Freeman?"

The questions gouged into him, and he didn't know what answer she expected. He had already answered them about going to Bill Jack's tonight. Maybe they hadn't understood. He shook his head.

Fred looked at Willna Mae and shook his head. He smiled at Freeman. The smile was forced and wavery. "Freeman, please?"

"Now stop this foolishness," she said. "You're going with us. You wouldn't let us go off without you, would you?"

Freeman looked at the toes of his shoes. This was all too sudden. "You can stay here," he said again.

Willna Mae said, "We tried that once. It didn't work. They surely knew we'd be coming back for you, if not to stay ourselves. And they've tried to hang onto you and make you so tied up with them that you wouldn't want to go."

Freeman wanted to deny the charge and explain to them what he only this minute knew for himself. Mom and Pop had kept a distance between Freeman and themselves because they knew he might have to make such a decision. They had refrained from too close an attachment because they knew the loneliness and hurt which could become his and theirs if separation came.

Mom and Pop were both leaning toward Freeman, looking as if they wanted to speak but could not.

"I'll stay here," he said.

"Freeman, come on." Willna's voice sounded impatient.

Freeman stiffened against the command and took a step nearer to Pop. He laid his hand on the chair, ready to hold onto it if anyone tried to force him to go.

"I wish things didn't have to be like this," Pop said. "Wish we could let bygones be done. Your bed's up there waiting. This is all happening so fast, and we're tired, all of us." Pop adjusted a doily on the chair arm, then absent-mindedly placed it on a table. "We all need to get a good night's sleep. Things'll look better tomorrow. They'll work out, you'll see."

Fred stood up, lifted his chair and set it nearer the

wall. "We promised Bill Jack we'd come up there tonight. He'll be expecting us." He bent down toward Freeman. "You're going with us?"

Freeman swallowed hard. He wanted to ask, "You're staying with us?" Instead, he said in a near whisper, "Not tonight."

Willna Mae came and squatted beside him. She held out her hands. She bent forward as if to kiss him, then changed her mind. "See you tomorrow then. Good night, Freeman."

"Good night." He looked up at Fred Sloan and said, "Good night."

When they were gone, Mom said, "Want to go to bed or stay up and talk?"

"I wish—" Freeman couldn't finish the sentence, and Mom didn't seem to expect it to be finished. Mae, Willie Mae, Willna Mae, would he ever be able to call her mother? Things might have been different if he'd known about them all these years. And they might have been the same. He yawned, then yawned again.

"Maybe you'd better get some rest. We'll talk tomorrow," Mom told him.

He walked past the extra bedroom, then went back. He turned on the light and looked about him. The room had always looked the same, clean and attractive. A tall-posted bed with a green spread, a chest with a white vase of feathers and artificial flowers, a dresser with a white bowl on one end. He tried to imagine Fred and Willna Mae Sloan here in the room, but he could not. He tried to imagine himself at Bill Jack Coleman's, and he couldn't do that either. He had found a father and a mother and lost them again. He was disappointed with them and with himself. Maybe he had expected too much, had expected a fairy-tale ending to the story: And the prisoner was released and became a handsome prince who moved into a castle with his princess and the young prince and they all lived happily ever after. Maybe some of it could work out, if they all tried.

He called, "Mom, is it all right if I put a hoop on the barn tomorrow for practicing basketball?"

"It's fine with me. Check with Pop."

The full moon outside the window looked as if he could reach out and pluck it from the sky, perhaps use it for a ball.

Freeman kicked off his shoes and leaned back on the bed. He drew up his feet and drew up his knees. He leaned forward until his chin was resting between his knees. He heard the pickup truck stop, heard the door slam. Old Lead and Stemper, barking to question this late activity, sounded far away and not really much concerned with it.

He knew he should go to his own room and undress for bed, but he couldn't seem to get up enough energy for doing so. He was sorry that he hadn't been able to make his mother and father understand how he felt about leaving Mom and Pop.

Maybe tomorrow he could begin by saying, "You see, they'd be lost without me. And this was too soon, too much like taking off with strangers. But we can stop being strangers. . . ."

And whatever he didn't get said tomorrow he could say the day after that and for days and days, maybe. There were so many things to hear and to tell. Things to teach and to learn. With a new beginning tomorrow.